THE BIG TIME

THE BIG TIME

HOLLYWOOD HEARTS
BOOK 2

IAN O. LEWIS

EDITED BY
ANN ATTWOOD

 Cruz PUBLISHING

For Kitty Carpenter- I miss you every single day

CHAPTER 1

CHRIS

"I wonder how much money I'd make donating sperm?"

Since Hugo had moved out, money was tight. The picture of a smiling couple cradling an infant next to the sign for the sperm bank was reassuring. Not only could I make a little cash, I could help a couple struggling to have a child achieve their dream.

"Fuck it, I don't have anything to lose." With a shaking hand I pushed open the glass double doors and strolled into a frigid waiting room. I rubbed my arms, trying to get warm. Three men were seated on beige plastic chairs, with several seats in between them. Moments later, a dude with long brown hair in braids strolled into the room carrying a little plastic container with a huge grin stretched across his face. He went to the front desk and handed it to a nurse, who yawned and thanked him. She looked like she'd rather be anywhere else than here. Must be a boring job collecting sperm samples, especially when you didn't have to extract it yourself.

It must be bizarre knowing that strange men were in that

little room where that dude was, jerking off into a plastic container. Lord knows I'd be making up all kinds of stories about them in my head while…

"Sir, how may I help you?" The nurse muttered, organizing papers on her desk at the same time.

"Um, well, I was wondering about…"

"Here," she handed me a glossy brochure with a baby's grinning red face on the front. "This is all the information you need. Read it over, and if you are still interested call the number on the back to set up an appointment." She spun around on her chair and began stuffing folders into a file cabinet.

"Sure, thanks." I muttered, then felt a flush of embarrassment race up my neck. Did I really want dozens of mini-me's growing up in Los Angeles? Hell, I'd do anything to pay the rent, and with Hugo gone, I was struggling. I hurried to the door, and when I was back out on the sidewalk realized I'd been holding my breath. Leaning against the building for a moment, I watched an older man in his thirties practically skipping into the sperm bank. He was probably excited to go jerk one out on his lunch hour.

"How did things get so fucking bad?"

———

As I fumbled for my keys, the door to the apartment across from mine opened, and a homely dude walked out, followed by my neighbor. The dude was my age, with a smattering of zits on his left cheek, and curly black hair cut short.

"Can we do this again?" The guy asked, pecking my neighbor on the lips and slapping his ass. *How the hell does my neighbor, who must be in his mid-sixties with dyed black hair and a pencil-thin mustache, get lucky all the time?* He was only wearing a shiny black robe with a picture of a tiger printed on it.

"You know the rules, Enrique. One and done, but trust me, you were perfect." My neighbor replied, then I slid my key in the lock and hurried inside. Just as I was going to flip on the lights there was a knock at my door.

"Who the hell is it?" I muttered, then dread washed through me. My neighbor, I could lay money on it. I peeked through the peephole, and saw my intuition was correct. There was something extra sleazy about this guy. When he'd hang out by the pool wearing nothing but a neon-colored thong, everyone avoided him. Plus he reeked of tacky drugstore cologne. Reluctantly, I pulled the door open and attempted a smile.

"Hi, my name is Billy Higgins." The man grinned and held his hand out. I shook his damp palm once and let it drop. "We're neighbors, and I was hoping you could help me out with something."

Jesus, I hope he wasn't expecting me to do whatever Enrique had just done. "Um, depends on what it is." I stepped into the hallway and shut the door, hoping to discourage Billy from wanting to go inside my place.

"I'm flying to the coast tomorrow for a few days." Billy's eyes dropped to my waist, then slowly worked their way up my body. I shuddered, then hoped he hadn't noticed.

"Um, that's nice." I said, wondering why people on the west coast always assumed you knew which coast they were referring to.

Billy licked his lips, his tongue briefly covering his mustache. "I was hoping you could keep an eye on my place, since it's right across the hall. More importantly I was hoping you could collect my mail every day that I'm gone." He stuck his hand in the pocket of his robe and pulled out two twenty dollar bills. Shit, I was so desperate for cash I'd do just about anything. The door to the stairs at the end of the hallway flew open just then, and the breeze made Billy's robe nearly come undone.

Hell no. I won't do that.

I eyed the money, then snatched it out of his hand.

"Here's the key to the mailbox." He held the key out, and I reluctantly took it. "Thank you very much. What is your name, young man?" Billy winked.

"Chris." I forced a smile. "Sorry, but I have to go and um, get dressed for an event." I lied, then I turned and opened my door. His hand clamped onto my shoulder, and I froze.

"This is my card, and you can reach me at this number." Billy said, so I turned again, took the card, and went inside, shutting the door before he could say anything else. I leaned against the door, and a fit of giggles hit me.

"Jesus, he's so sleazy. I can only imagine what he and those young dudes get up to." I whispered, then wondered if they were prostitutes. Flipping the business card over, I noticed it only had his name, Billy Higgins, and a phone number. Whatever his business was, it apparently wasn't important enough to put on a card. I turned on the overhead lights, then my phone buzzed. I pulled it out of my pocket and saw a text from Mom.

> I saw you on the cover of another romance novel 😀

"Shit." I sighed, then strolled into the living room and fell back on the couch. Everyone thought I was a brilliant success thanks to those romance covers, but I made no money off of them. When I first arrived in Hollywood I'd been hired by a photographer to model for her. It was the first bit of cash I'd made from modeling, but it was a one-off deal, with no royalties. The woman apparently posted the photos on stock photo sites online, and made all the money. It was too bad, since my mug was on the cover of over a dozen novels and counting.

"Hell, maybe I need to accept the fact that I've failed. Making it in Hollywood was just a pipedream..." I hit the pillow next to me, grateful that Hugo had left all of his furniture. Now that he lived in a fucking beachside mansion, he didn't need this cheap stuff. "...and accept the fact that I might be heading home to Richmond with my tail tucked between my legs."

My phone pinged again, but I didn't have the heart to chat with Mom or anyone else. Something bad must have happened, because all of my modeling and acting gigs seemed to dry up at once. If only I could figure out what went wrong. It had been almost two months since my last job, and if something didn't change fast, I'd either be living in one of the homeless camps downtown on Skid Row, or hitchhiking back to Virginia.

I didn't have many options. My agent seemed to have vanished off the face of the earth, and it was virtually impossible to get work in Hollywood without one. I could get a job waiting tables, but I totally sucked at it. I'd had three jobs as a waiter over the years, and I'd been fired from every one of them within a month of starting. Now I was contemplating donating blood or sperm. Hell, maybe I should swallow my pride and knock on old sleazy Billy's door. I was a helluva lot better looking than most of the guys trooping in and out of his place.

The lights flickered out.

"What the fuck?"

I reached beside me to switch on a lamp, but it didn't work. Then I realized how quiet it was. The usual hum of the refrigerator and air conditioning was gone.

"Oh hell," I moaned, then picked up my phone. "Fuck me." There was a message from the electric company. My power was shut off due to non-payment. My arm swung back, ready to slam the phone into the wall, but somehow I stopped myself. I swiped a tear from the side of my nose, then burrowed down into the cushions.

"What the hell am I going to do now?"

CHAPTER 2
JETT

"I think I'm going to be sick," I muttered while struggling to get the bathroom window open. My eyes watered, and I could barely breathe. After another push, the ancient wood finally budged, and a stream of chilly fresh air streamed into the bathroom.

I lived in the basement of an ancient house in Oregon Hill, one of the few in the neighborhood that hadn't been renovated, which was why I was able to afford it. Unfortunately, it meant wiping down the walls of the bathroom every month with a bleach solution to kill mold and mildew. If I didn't my voice would suffer.

"Can't have that." I stuck my head out the window for a moment, inhaling fresh air.

"Hi Jett." My upstairs neighbor leaned down and grinned at me from the sidewalk. Mike was a bartender at the local gay bar, Thirsty's. I waved, then backed out of the bathroom into the bedroom, and threw myself onto the mattress in the corner. I couldn't afford a bed, and the few items of furniture I possessed came from the surrounding alleys. Nevertheless, I was thrilled about one thing.

For the first time ever, I paid my bills entirely with my music.

I grabbed my phone and clicked on TikTok. According to them, I now had 37k followers, and made a little over three hundred bucks there last month. Combine that with the cash I made with streaming services like Spotify, and live performances around Virginia; I cleared more money than I ever had before. It wasn't much, but it was enough to pay all my bills doing what I loved the most—writing and performing music.

The problem was how long it was taking to build up a fan base, and living in Richmond, Virginia wasn't helping matters any. I needed to be in New York, or LA. That was where all the action was, where I could connect with people in the industry who could help me break into the big time.

I clicked on Instagram, and the first picture on my screen was Chris. He was my ex-boyfriend, though we hadn't dated for long. We went to the same private school in the west end, and the summer after graduation was when our brief affair started. Who knew what could have been between us, because we knew from the start that once summer ended and I moved to Boston, it would be over. Both of us were ambitious, and he totally understood why I had to go to Berklee College of Music. Chris knew he wanted to be a model and an actor, and a couple of years after graduation he left Richmond for Los Angeles. I was the stupid one who came back home, when I should've moved to New York after I got my degree.

"You are still easy on the eyes, Chris." I tapped on picture after picture on his profile, relishing the memory of his touch. He'd been my first, and he claimed I'd been his. Our school was small, and neither of us had felt comfortable coming out until after graduation.

"Jesus, you're sex on a stick." I muttered. This picture was taken on a beach in LA. He was tall, muscular, but without being an overdeveloped muscle freak. His green eyes popped next to his tan skin, and Chris's dark-blond hair was blowing in the breeze. But what I noticed most was the bulge in his tight blue swim suit.

"Damn it, my career isn't going anywhere in this fucking town." I clicked off the phone and forced myself to my feet. Every afternoon I roamed the streets of Richmond taking pics and videos for social media. Hell, TikTok was almost a full-time job in itself. I resented the amount of time I spent on self-promotion, because it took me away from what I loved most —music.

My leather jacket had fallen off the beat-up chair I'd rescued from a dumpster, so I snatched it from the floor and slid it on. Then I grinned at my reflection in the broken mirror next to the front door, making sure I looked presentable enough to take more pics and vids of myself. My wavy brown hair scraped my shoulders, and I noticed a tiny zit sprouting on my chin. No problem. That was simple to filter out.

"Hi beautiful." I laughed, though it wasn't from joy. It was from nerves, from feeling like an imposter every time I posted yet another picture of myself. There was a blurry line between self-promotion and vanity, and I prayed I never, ever crossed it.

———

After shooting a video of me on a rock in the middle of the James River I was chilled to the bone, so I decided to grab a cup of coffee at Percolate. It was an LGBTQ friendly coffee house that featured occasional concerts by local artists, and I'd played there myself a handful of times.

On my walk up Laurel Street, I passed the tall, fancy apartment building my landlord Michael owned. A few of my friends lived there, but I could never afford it myself. It was sleek, sophisticated, and filled with successful lawyers and doctors, with a sprinkling of successful musicians and artists. They had what I wanted, success. If I didn't figure out a way forward with my career soon, I'd end up living in moldy basements for the rest of my life.

"Jett!" One of my favorite people in the world yelled at me from a block away.

"Sneaky!" I threw my arms around her. "It's been way too long." She pushed me back and eyed me.

"I heard a song of yours on Spotify while cleaning the bar last night." She brushed imaginary lint off my jacket and grinned. "Somebody's making a name for himself. Are you heading toward Cary Street?"

"Yeah, I'm grabbing a cup of joe at Percolate."

She took my arm in hers and started dragging me up the street. "I'm going to work, so let's keep each other company."

Sneaky was a fixture in Oregon Hill, and owned a bar next door to the coffee shop. I'd also performed at her bar before, but now I was hitting a stage in my career where playing live at small local venues didn't pay what I was worth. Recently I'd been making the trek up to Washington DC every couple of weeks to play bigger venues, like the 9:30 Club.

"How's Gabe?" I asked about her husband, a disc jockey at a local radio station. He'd been incredibly helpful getting my music out there when I first began recording.

"Oh, he's planning some sort of show on Brown's Island for April." We turned onto Cary Street, and were steps away from her bar. "Would you be interested in performing? He didn't ask me to ask you, but you've played so many gigs with him that I thought you might want to." She let go of me and started digging in her backpack, then whipped out a set of keys.

"I'm not sure what's happening over the next few weeks." I sighed. "Tell Gabe to shoot me an email with the details, and I'll check my calendar."

"Is something wrong?" She stuck her key in the lock, jiggled it a few times, and the door popped open. "You don't sound like yourself."

"I've got a lot on my mind." I pecked her on the cheek. "If the coffee doesn't warm me up, I might stop in for a drink later."

"Please, do." She swiped her black curls off her forehead, and I noticed a small teardrop tattooed under her eye, which must be a new one. Lord knows she didn't have any other available skin left to adorn. "The college kids have been drinking at that new bar over on Floyd Avenue, and I would love the company."

When I pushed open the door to Percolate, a blast of warm air hit me. Then I noticed a young woman on the tiny stage tuning a guitar.

"Hey, Jett. Over here!" I heard a man's voice, then saw Josh and Serge seated in a booth toward the rear of the coffee house. I held up a finger, and mouthed, "Give me a minute," then got in line to get a cup of coffee. A few moments later I slid into the booth next to Serge. He was one of my idols, a man who made his living completely off of music, though in an entirely different genre. He was the conductor of the Richmond Symphony, and Josh, his husband, was a cellist. "Hey guys, what's up?"

Josh opened his mouth to answer, but the woman on stage began strumming her guitar. Like all musicians, the three of us stopped talking and paid attention, while most of the audience kept murmuring to themselves. People were totally fucking rude, and I made a mental note to leave her some money in the tip jar next to the stage. She was a decent singer, though folk music wasn't my jam. It was a little too hippy-dippy for me, but I appreciated anyone with the nerve to put themselves out there. Half-an-hour later, she took a break, and Josh winked at me.

"What's wrong, Jett?" Josh raised his coffee cup to his lips, then set it down without drinking it. "You look like someone kicked your cat."

Jesus, my parents are right. I wore my feelings on my face, and couldn't lie my way out of a paper bag. "That singer reminds me of myself when I first started. The problem is that I'm beyond where she is right now, and I feel like I'm treading water here in Virginia."

"I don't listen to pop music very much, but maybe it's time to move." Serge sipped his tea, then made a face. It was probably cold.

"Move?" Josh raised an eyebrow. "Why should he move?"

Serge put his arm over my shoulder. "You went to one of the best music schools in the world, and you know the business. If you want to make it, like truly make it in pop music, you need to be where the action is. Los Angeles, or New York, though I'd opt for London. It's much more exciting there."

My phone buzzed, so I pulled it out of my pocket. A second later I heard Serge gasp. When I glanced at him, his eyes were trained on my phone. "Jett, you have almost forty thousand followers on TikTok. That's more than the symphony has."

"Wow." Josh snatched the phone out of my hand and began scrolling.

"And that's why my head is in a fucked-up place." I sighed. "Last month, I didn't have to work a single temp job. I paid every bill with my music, but I'm still living in a horrible basement eating ramen noodles for breakfast, lunch, and dinner."

"Time to move on." Serge's baritone rumbled. "Richmond's

perfect for me and Josh, but we're not in the pop-music world. If you want to take your career to the next level, you gotta move."

Josh handed me the phone back, and I switched from TikTok to Instagram. Chris's face filled the screen. He was mugging the camera with that celebrity buddy of his, Hugo something. Chris was doing alright in Hollywood, and I thought I saw him in an ad for tennis rackets a few months ago.

'Maybe you're right, Serge." I pointed at Chris's pic. "This is my ex, Chris Reynolds. We went to the same school here in Richmond. Now he's in California modeling and making commercials."

"Are you guys still friends?" Josh asked, raising a red eyebrow.

"Well, kind of." I shrugged. "We like each other's posts on social media, if that counts."

"You should contact him." Serge nodded toward me, and I realized he wanted out of the booth. I stood and let him up. When he was on his feet, he placed his hands on my shoulders and looked me square in the eye. "Maybe he can help you find a place to live, or a job while you figure out what to do next with your career." He let go of me and walked toward the restrooms.

My head swirled. Chris and I hadn't had a serious conversation in years. But what if he could help me out?

"Do you believe in yourself?" Josh asked, and I slid the phone back into my jacket pocket. If I'd gotten this far with my music, there was a slim chance that moving to Hollywood might put me in touch with the people who could really move my career forward.

"Yeah." I put my face in my hands and sighed. "The question is, will anyone else believe in me?"

• • •

CHAPTER 3

CHRIS

"If I pay the power bill, I won't be able to afford food." I sighed. "If I don't pay the power bill, I won't have a way to cook any food, damn it."

This situation was dire. Yes, I could call my parents and ask for a loan, and they wouldn't hesitate in sending enough money to get me by for a few weeks. But I was twenty-five years old, and going to my parents with my hand out wasn't cool.

I glanced at my phone, and it was now only nineteen percent charged. The coffee shop down the street would let me charge it there, but they'd probably frown when I didn't buy anything.

"This absolutely sucks donkey dicks." I flipped through my contacts, found my agent's number and placed the call. Cramer would tell me what was going on, and why I hadn't had a job in weeks. Even if I had to fire his ass for not doing his job, I needed to know what happened.

"Hello?" The old man's voice cracked. Something didn't

smell right about this, because he normally answered with Cramer Talent Agency.

"Cramer, it's Chris Reynolds." The room was growing dark, so I got up and opened the drapes. "Why haven't you booked me any work recently? Is there something wrong?"

"Chris?" The old man sounded confused. "I released you and all of my other talent weeks ago when I retired. Didn't Gerty send you the letter?"

"What?" I couldn't believe this. "No, I never got a letter, or anything else telling me that…"

"Damn it." Cramer sighed. "My secretary was angry that I closed up shop. You're the third client I've heard from who didn't get notice of my retirement. She did it to get back at me, I swear."

I hit the sofa arm with my fist. "What the hell am I supposed to do now? Like, I'm sitting in the fucking dark because I can't pay the power bill."

"I'm very sorry, Chris. After I retired I moved to Salt Lake City to be near my family, so I'm not even close to the action. If there was anything I could do for you, I promise I would do it." Cramer's voice trembled, or my phone was about to die. The man wasn't fucking me over on purpose, because he looked like he'd been working in Hollywood since before the talkies. The only reason I accepted him as an agent was because no one else was interested in repping me.

"Okay," I sighed. "At least now I know what's going on. Enjoy your retirement, Cramer." I disconnected the call before it became even more uncomfortable.

What the hell was happening? I had no money, no upcoming work, and I might end up jerking off into plastic cups so I could make rent if something didn't change, and fast. I glanced out the window, and saw orange and purple streaks in the sky. If I was going to charge my phone at the coffee shop, I'd better do it now before it got dark.

I pushed myself off the couch, then hit my shin on the coffee table.

"Fuck!" I screamed, and someone knocked at the door. "Hell, knowing my luck it's my pervy neighbor." I hobbled to the door and threw it open.

"Chris, what's wrong?" Hugo crossed his arms over his chest and looked at me like I had two heads.

"What are you doing...? Scratch that, come in." I stepped back, then Hugo walked past me and attempted to flip on the lights.

"Um, your lights don't seem to be..."

"The power company shut off service." I groaned, shutting the door. "Today has been the worst day of my life. My agent retired, so I haven't gotten work in weeks. Then I came home and the power went out." I fingered the two twenty dollar bills in my pocket. "Like I have less than fifty dollars to my name, and I don't know what the hell I'm going to do."

Hugo opened the drapes even wider, then strolled into the kitchen and came back with two lit candles on saucers. "The reason I'm here is I left a box of cookbooks somewhere, and I wanted to get them. But you're in trouble, so let's get you taken care of first." Hugo placed the candles on the coffee table, and pointed at the couch. "Sit."

I flopped down on the couch, and Hugo whipped out his phone and started typing. Seconds later it rang, then he answered.

"Marla, Chris is in big trouble."

———

"Have you told Chris the news yet?" Marla sat in between Hugo and me on the couch and opened her briefcase.

"News?" I shrugged. "What's up, Hugo?"

"I figured I'd wait to tell you until after we figured out this mess, but the tabloids will probably find out soon anyway." Hugo grinned and waggled his eyebrows. "Becks and I are getting married in Mexico City next year, and you're going to be my best man."

"I am?" Wow. Oh, I'm supposed to congratulate him. "Oh, Hugo, that's awesome news." I felt like I should hug him, but I was too exhausted to move. "Yeah, I'll be your best man, as long as I'm not homeless or something."

"Aww, sweetie, chin up!" Marla smiled, then opened her laptop. "Do you have a copy of your power bill? I'm going to pay it for you, and you should consider it an advance."

"An advance?" What on earth did she mean?

"Hugo's career is blowing up, and I want to grow my stable of talent." Marla pushed her glasses up her nose, then began typing away. I found the account number for the power company on my phone and handed it to her. A moment later, she shut the laptop and patted my knee. "It's paid. They say it will be turned back on within twenty-four hours. Do you want to stay with me or Hugo tonight?"

"Oh no, I don't want to put either of you out." I fell back against the cushions and stared at the ceiling. "How did I let things get so bad?"

"So what happened with your agent?" Marla asked, then Hugo got up and padded into the kitchen.

I told her about the phone call with Cramer, and Marla shook her head slowly back and forth.

"That's so unprofessional. No wonder your career wasn't going very far." Marla said. "Tell me about the work you've done, and don't leave anything out, especially if it's embarrassing. I'll represent anyone, unless they've done porn."

I snickered. "Things haven't gotten that desperate yet." Hugo walked in with another lit candle on a saucer. "Well, maybe I am at the bottom. No porn. Mostly modeling work, catalog stuff. For two years I had steady work with Nordstrom, modeling for their catalogs. Last year I started getting commercials, including one for Babolat tennis rackets. Shit, why haven't I gotten any residuals for that yet?"

"You might need to have an audit done on your last agent. Sounds like someone wasn't paying you what you were owed." Marla tapped on her phone. "I'm emailing you the contact info for my attorney. They should be able to handle it for you, and they're reasonable. For lawyers, that is. So, where do you see your career going? Like, tell me your ambitions."

I shrugged. "In high school I was in the drama club, and thought I wanted to be an actor. Then I was scouted by the Wilhelmina modeling agency in New York before I graduated, and thought that was the direction I should go in. But after interviewing them, I decided against it. I didn't feel comfortable with them, so I took a chance and came to LA."

"Would you be open to acting classes?" Marla blew a lock of burgundy hair off her forehead. "The real money is in acting. With your looks, even if you're not super-talented, we can get you noticed."

"Well, yeah. I kept telling Cramer I wanted more acting gigs, but he kept tossing me modeling jobs." I murmured, then wondered for the first time if I'd made a huge mistake signing with the old man. "It's like I was treading water the whole time I was signed with him. I made enough money to pay the rent, and thought that was pretty successful. At least I wasn't waiting tables as a side gig."

"Okay, I need your promise that you'll trust me." Marla

pulled a folder out of her briefcase and squinted at the sheets in the candlelight. "I can get you some great modeling gigs right off the bat, but I know we can make you a successful actor if you're prepared to work hard for it." She pulled a pen out of her bag and handed it to me. "I want to sign you up for acting classes, which will come out of your pay, along with the electric bill. I take fifteen percent of your gross, and as you can see with my little brother, I'm worth every penny. It will take a little time to start the wheels turning, so you will need to come up with a part-time job for a few weeks. Get a roommate too, to help with expenses. Hopefully you won't need a side gig for very long."

Marla held out the papers for me to sign, and I prayed I was doing the right thing. I took them from her, and scrawled my name on the dotted line.

"When's the last time you had headshots taken?" She took the pen and contract from me and stuffed them in her briefcase.

"When I first arrived in LA, so it was maybe five years ago?" I couldn't remember.

"We'll have new ones taken, pronto. I'm positive you don't look the same way you did when you first showed up on the scene." She stood and held her hand out to help me to my feet. "It's the same photographer Hugo uses, so the quality is top-notch. Hugo, do you need a ride?"

Hugo stood and grinned. "No, I drove. Chris, why don't you spend the night with me and Becks. We've got three guest rooms, so you aren't putting us out. It's too depressing in this dark apartment."

Hm. Beachfront mansion for the night, or sitting alone in the dark here? I swallowed my pride and answered him. "Thanks, Hugo. Yes, I'll spend the night. Let me grab a few things out of my bedroom, then we'll take off."

I took a candle from the table and hurried into my bedroom. "Well now, things are definitely looking up," I muttered while stuffing my backpack with my phone charger, a pair of shorts, and a t-shirt. Then I felt my phone ping in my pocket. "Shit, I thought you'd died already." I pulled it out, and saw a message from someone I hadn't spoken to in years.

> Hey Chris, it's Jett. I know it's been a long time, but can we talk?

CHAPTER 4

JETT- TWO WEEKS LATER

"Why don't you move home, Jeffrey?" Mom pleaded, calling me by my birth name. "Instead of flying off to California where you don't have family or friends. We're going to worry about you." She swiped at her eyes with the back of her hand, while Dad just shook his head muttering curses under his breath. She'd bitched about my moving to Hollywood incessantly since I told them about it two weeks ago. Now that I was at the airport waiting for my flight, she was determined to change my mind.

"Mom, I already told you I'm staying with a friend from Steward School, Chris Reynolds. Don't you remember him?"

"Of course she does." Dad spat. "I work with Chris's father, and he brags about his precious boy whenever he shows up on one of those silly romance novel covers." Dad wasn't a patient man, and whenever Mom tried to guilt him or me about anything, he'd be snippy. "Beth, please, Jeffrey is old enough to make his own decisions, so stop with the guilt trip."

Dad was the easier of the two to get along with. As long as I had a roof over my head and food in my belly, he was fine. We looked alike, except his brown hair had streaks of gray, and as the years passed, he'd developed a barrel chest. Mom, on the other hand, was a control freak. I suspected she didn't care if I was on the other side of the country. What she wanted was to be the center of attention. If that involved criticizing me, or making me feel guilty about anything, that was fine by her. Despite that, she'd been a fierce supporter of me and my musical career. She just wished I'd pursue it from the confines of the family home.

I glanced out the enormous window and stared for a moment at the swarm of airport employees removing luggage from an airplane. Flying wasn't my favorite thing to do, and I'd contemplated renting a car and driving across the country instead. It wasn't natural for a hunk of metal weighing several tons to fly through the air. But a cheap, one-way ticket to Los Angeles was far less expensive than a week-long cross-country trip.

"Excuse me," An older man with dyed black hair and a pencil-thin mustache waved his hand at the bored flight attendant standing at the gate. "How much longer do we have to wait for the flight to LA?"

The older woman grimaced, though I thought she imagined she was smiling. She pointed behind her, tilting her head. "It's on time. See. Right there, on the screen."

"Hm." The man spun around and sat a few seats away from us. "Somebody's having a bad day."

"Are you sure you have enough money?" Mom opened her hot-pink purse, and Dad glared at her.

"Yes, Mom. Since my lease was up, I didn't have to pay rent this month, and I'm publishing another single on the streaming sites this week." I replied, then realized I should take pics for social media. My followers ate this sort of thing up, so I pulled my phone out and took a few shots of the terminal. Then I held the phone away from me and leaned into Mom. "Smile." I said, and Mom did as I asked. Seconds later the photos were on Instagram.

"I just don't understand the constant need to post your personal life all over the internet." Dad sniffed.

"It's for business, Dad. Fans like to know what it's like to be…"

"Flight 64A from Richmond International Airport to LAX is now boarding." The flight attendant muttered into the microphone. "First class passengers come forward please."

"You have to call us as soon as you land." Mom and Dad rose to their feet, and I hugged both of them.

"Of course, Mom." I felt pressure behind my eyes, and resisted the urge to cry. The fear of failure weighed heavily on me. What if I arrived in LA and realized I'd made a huge mistake?

———

Of course the sleazy-looking dude with the weird mustache had the seat next to me in the rear of the plane. And because it was economy, we were squished together. Every time he or I crossed our legs or changed position we'd touch, and he wasn't the sort of man I wanted touching me. For the first half of the flight he read a book on an e-reader, but once the Rocky Mountains were underneath us, he turned his charm on me.

"As soon as I walked into the terminal I noticed you." He murmured, and when I turned to him he winked. "You have a handsome face, and a great smile. Are you an actor?"

I didn't want to encourage him, but he hadn't said anything inappropriate. Yet.

"No, I'm not an actor." I focussed on my phone, hoping he'd get the hint and leave me alone.

"My mistake." The man chuckled, and I realized who he reminded me of. That funny film director, John Waters, except he was sleazier. "My name is Billy, and I'm always looking for fresh talent. Are you coming to LA for vacation?"

How could I get this man to shut up without being rude? "No, I'm moving to West Hollywood." I said, then added, "My boyfriend lives there." No, I didn't have a boyfriend, but maybe he'd leave me alone if he thought I was taken. The man's grin grew wider.

"Of course, somebody as attractive as you wouldn't be single." Billy crossed his leg, accidentally kicking my shin. "Oops, sorry about that."

I stood up and opened the overhead bin. After digging through my backpack I found my black velvet sleep mask and slid it over my head. "No problem. I'm going to take a nap." I sank back into the seat and pulled the mask down over my eyes.

"Sweet dreams." Billy murmured.

—————

"Ladies and gentleman, we are now beginning our descent to LAX." The flight attendant coughed, then continued. "Please ensure that your seatbelt is securely fastened, your seat back and tray table are in their upright and locked positions, and your carry-on luggage is stowed underneath the seat in front of you or in the overhead compartment."

I removed the sleep mask and buckled up, then Billy handed me a card.

"If you're ever in need of extra cash, give me a call." He grinned, and I noticed his forehead didn't move. Well, I was moving to the land of botox. I glanced at the card, and it only had the man's name and phone number.

"Um, thanks." I stuffed the card in the pocket of my jeans, and the plane began to shake.

"Is this your first time flying?" Billy asked. "You're clutching the armrest like we're about to die."

'No, I just hate flying. The landing is my least favorite part." I muttered through gritted teeth. What I didn't say was how nervous I was to see Chris again. When he called and said he had an extra bedroom I could crash in, the sound of his voice took me back to our school days. Chris and I had been in the drama club, and because it was a small school, we were in almost every class together. He hadn't been a brain, and neither was I. Both of us had plans for the future that involved the arts, so academic success wasn't a goal for either of us.

I'd always suspected he was gay, but neither of us had been out to our classmates. The day after graduation we went to a party together at a classmate's house. After a few beers we left, and spent a long night talking about our dreams while drinking cup after cup of coffee at Aunt Sarah's Pancake House. Then we both confessed that we preferred people with penises instead of vajayjays, and a brief, whirlwind romance began.

"I wonder if we would've stayed together." I whispered, then the plane shuddered one last time and came to a halt.

"Thank you for choosing to fly with JetBlue airlines. Enjoy your stay in Los Angeles, and we look forward to seeing you again." The attendant said, and I popped out of my seat to get my bag out of the overhead compartment.

"Would you mind handing me the red bag?" Billy grinned up at me. His bag was made from some bright, shiny fabric. When I handed it to him our fingers touched, and I almost jumped. "Remember to call me if you're looking for work. You'd be perfect."

I had no idea what I'd be perfect at with him, but I suspected it was sketchy. "Yeah, sure. Have a great day." I

nearly ran the people in front of me over trying to get away
from Billy. Finally I was on the airbridge, and it hit me that I
was about to see my ex-boyfriend for the first time in years. I
prayed I didn't look horrible from my flight. But then again,
who didn't look bad, unless you flew first class.

"Jett!"

Oh my God. I froze, and a small child ran into the back of
my legs.

"Amanda, come back here!" A woman yelled, and I forced
my feet forward. Standing not twenty feet away was the most
handsome man I'd ever laid eyes on. Of course I'd stalked
Chris on social media already, but the reality of him was sooo
much better. He was a model for a reason, with a sharp nose,
full lips, and wavy dark-blond hair. Why did we break up
again? School for me, and Hollywood for him. As soon as I was
in front of Chris I glanced up to stare into his sparkling green
eyes. What was the etiquette for reuniting with an ex? Did we
hug, or shake hands? I held my hand out, and Chris pulled me
into his chest and squeezed. My eyes shut, and his woodsy
citrus scent filled my nostrils.

"It's good to see you man." Chris murmured, still not letting
go of me. "I can't wait for us to…"

"Did I ask you to meet me at the airport?" A man's voice
killed the moment. Chris let go, and I turned around. Of course,
it was the sleazy guy. Was he talking to one of us?

"Billy?" Chris put his hands on his hips. "What are you
doing here?"

How the hell did Chris know this guy?

"I flew back from the coast, and here you are." Billy winked,
and pointed at Chris. "So, is this the boyfriend you told me
about on the plane?"

CHAPTER 5

JETT

wanted the ground to open up and swallow me.

"Boyfriend?" Chris cocked an eyebrow at Billy, then his back stiffened. "Me?" He pointed at his chest, then his eyes widened. "Oh, yes. This is my boyfriend Jett, Billy. God, I'm so glad he's moving in. We've known each other for years." Chris winked at me and threw his arm around my shoulder. Thank God he understood why I made up the boyfriend part. I was sure this Billy guy was nice, but he kinda gave me the creeps.

"Well, if you weren't here to pick me up, how about we share a taxi back to our apartment building." Billy grinned.

"Jett, Billy is my neighbor. He lives across the hall from me, well, now it's us." Chris's green eyes locked with mine, then he brushed his lips across my cheek. Dizziness washed through me, and I realized I wasn't breathing. "Yeah, let's share a cab. I've got to give you your mail anyways. Oh, and some young guy named Frankie keeps knocking on my door, wondering when you are getting back."

"Oh, bless his heart." Billy began walking out of the terminal, so we followed along behind him. "I told him it's a one and done deal, but he wants more." He spoke over his shoulder. I glanced up at Chris who shrugged. "Poor kid. He told me he was kicked out of his house as a teenager, and he does all sorts of odd jobs for cash. Let's grab our luggage, boys."

"You did the right thing telling Billy we're boyfriends." Chris whispered in my ear, and the hairs on the back of my neck pricked up. "He has all sorts of sketchy dudes over, and I'm wondering if they're hustlers."

"Hustlers?" I whispered back.

"You know, prostitutes." Chris leaned down and whispered, and his breath smelled like mints. "I mean, would you want to sleep with him for free?"

"You've got a point." I mumbled.

"Frankie has a good heart though, and I was glad to help him out." Billy said, and we arrived at the luggage carousel. Billy snagged a hot-pink leopard-print suitcase off of it, and I found my two suitcases and my guitar.

"Here, let me grab one of those for you." Chris picked up my black suitcase and made a face. "What's in here? Rocks?"

"No, that's my equipment." I slung the guitar case over my shoulder. "Laptops, keyboards, and cameras." It scared me to death flying my equipment cross country. Literally my life savings were crammed into my luggage, and if any of it was damaged, I was screwed.

"Come along, boys." Billy smiled at us and made a beeline for the exit. The glass doors to the airport slid open and Billy hurried through them with us a few feet behind him.

As soon as we were outside a woman began screaming at her kids to get in the damned car now. Jesus, LAX was massive compared to the Richmond airport. People were bumping into each other, cursing and yelling. I thought this was supposed to be a happy place, the entertainment capital of the world.

"Taxi!" Billy waved his arm in the air and a yellow car

pulled up to the curb. The trunk popped open and we stored our luggage inside, then the three of us piled into the backseat. Chris gave the elderly driver the address, and she inched the car into traffic.

I was stuck in the middle, and after a couple of minutes I felt heat against my thigh. Glancing down, I noticed Chris's muscular leg pressed hard against mine. Damn, I loved the feel of him, but perhaps I was enjoying it a little too much. I shut my eyes and instantly the memory of us at Byrd park filled my brain. We'd go there at night after drinking way too much coffee, talking about our plans for the future. Then, in the light of the full moon Chris took me in his arms and…

"What do you do Jett?" Billy's bony thigh pressed into mine, and my eyes reluctantly opened. "I saw a guitar case, so I'm guessing you're a musician, right?"

"Yeah."

"Yet another artist coming to Hollyweird, praying that the riches of Tinseltown will rain down on him." Billy yawned, and suddenly his arm was over my shoulders. "This town chews artists up and spits them out, unless you have that indescribable magic that catches an audience's attention and keeps it."

The driver yelled back, "I've been an actress for almost forty years. The most success I've had is driving this fucking cab."

"How about you, Chris?" I turned to him and he grinned. "Have things been looking up since you landed that new agent?"

"Marla is wonderful." His thigh pressed harder against mine. "Tomorrow I have a photo-shoot with a major sunglasses company, and the next day I'm auditioning for a Netflix movie. I doubt I'll get that job, but she says the more auditions I go on, the better I'll get."

I forced a smile. A muscular thigh and a skinny old one was

pressing into me at the same time. Very confusing signals that my hormones weren't able to process right now.

"I'm sure you'll do great." Billy reached over me and patted Chris's leg. "You've got the look that the cameras love. Trust me, I know about these things." I noticed a thin white line against Billy's scalp and realized he had a very bad dye job. Either that or hair plugs.

The cab passed a row of cute bungalows, then what appeared to be a six-story old apartment building came into view. Very generic, but nice.

"Home sweet home." Billy patted my thigh, a little too close to my junk. "I travel for work sometimes when I can't find decent local talent."

"Were you working in Richmond?" Chris asked. "Both Jett and I are from there."

"No wonder I find both of you boys to be so attractive. Richmond is a lovely city, but no. I was working in Norfolk. I saved a chunk of change flying out of Richmond."

"We're here." The driver stopped in front of the building, then we piled out of the car. I stared up at the tan-colored bricks for a moment, and thought, *Wow, this is absolutely nothing like home.* Palm trees lined the sidewalk, and an ocean-scented breeze ruffled my hair. A new adventure was beginning, and I fucking couldn't wait for it to start.

"I can't believe I'm really here, in Hollywood." I murmured, then Chris handed me the guitar and one of the suitcases.

Billy graciously paid the woman for the three of us, and we went inside. Chris pressed the button on the elevator and the doors slid open.

"After you," Chris gestured toward Billy who stepped inside and pushed a button. A few moments later the doors opened and Billy clucked his tongue.

"Look at that." He gestured toward one of the doors which

was covered in taped messages. He snatched one off the door and read it, his lips moving at the same time. "Poor Frankie. How the hell was he getting in the building? I never told him the code."

"I didn't tell him, and none of this was on your door when I left for the airport." Chris put the suitcases down and grabbed his keys out of his pocket. "Sorry, Billy. Thanks for paying for the cab. We'll see you later." His green eyes swept down my frame. "We've got a lot of catching up to do."

"Thanks for everything, Chris." Billy kissed his index finger and waved it at both of us.

A moment later we stepped inside and Chris flipped on the overhead lights. "As you can see, this is the living room, and the kitchen is this way." We left the bags on the floor and he walked me through the apartment. "We had a fully stocked kitchen, but my former roommate, Hugo, took most of the pots and pans." He opened the fridge and pulled out two beers, handing me one of them. "Let me show you your bedroom."

We walked down a dark hallway, then he opened a door and gestured for me to enter first. "You're lucky Hugo didn't need any furniture when he moved. He only took his personal belongings."

A queen-sized bed took up much of the space, and there was a simple chest of drawers underneath an open window. I slowly spun around taking it all in. "Chris, I'm so grateful for this. I just want you to know that I'm good for rent and bills. My music has been slowly taking off, and hopefully being here will…"

"I've heard your music, Jett." Chris stepped back until he filled the doorway. "It's amazing. Just like you. I'm wondering if my agent might be interested in repping you. She's been taking on a bunch of new clients lately, and trust me, you've got the goods to impress her."

Heat radiated through my chest. Did he really mean it? "Thanks," I mumbled. "I guess I should start unpacking my…"

"Hell no." Chris turned and padded down the hallway. What did he mean, no? I followed behind, then Chris muttered, "Shit."

"What?"

"I forgot to give Billy his mail."

He crossed the room and picked up a stack of plain brown envelopes. "It's kinda creepy. None of these have a return address, except for this one from Blackmagic."

"Blackmagic? Do you mean the video equipment company?" I stood next to him and peered at the envelopes. "Yeah, I use their camera for streaming live performances. Mostly from my bedroom, unfortunately."

Chris tilted his head and cocked an eye at me.

"What?"

"I can't believe I'm asking this, but…forget about it." Chris headed toward the front door and opened it.

"What were you going to ask me?"

"It's stupid." Chris bit his lower lip. "Are you on OnlyFans? Because they make serious money, and, well, you've definitely got the looks for it."

CHAPTER 6
CHRIS

"OnlyFans?" Jett shrugged. "Is that another streaming platform for musicians?"

Oh my God. Did Jett not know about OnlyFans? If so, he was possibly the only gay guy on the planet who didn't know about the porn paradise. Should I tell him? Nah. His innocence was about to be destroyed by Hollywood, and I didn't want to hasten the destruction.

"Um, let me get this mail to Billy." I mumbled, then hurried across the hall and knocked on Billy's door.

I could hear footsteps running on a hardwood floor. The door flew open, and Billy winked at me as he stepped through the doorway. He held two cupcakes wrapped in cellophane. The pink frosting was punctuated by colorful sprinkles.

"I knew it was you." Billy stepped back and nodded for me to enter. "Here's some cupcakes for you and that dishy boyfriend of yours."

"And here's your mail." I laid the envelopes on the entry table, then took the cupcakes from him. Hm. There's no way he just cooked these, which meant they had been sitting in his refrigerator for days while he was out of town. These wouldn't be eaten.

"You're like a work of art, Chris. I can't help but admire you." Billy waggled his eyebrows, and I noticed he'd changed into a pair of very skimpy shorts and a striped t-shirt cut off below his pecs.

"Thanks." I shrugged. "I guess I'll get back to..."

"Don't be so hasty young man." Billy took my arm and dragged me into the living room.

"Oh, wow." I grinned, trying not to laugh. A neon pink sofa with leopard-print cushions, velvet curtains with sequin trimmings, and a shag-pile carpet in rainbow stripes adorned the floor. The walls were lined with tacky art pieces, including a cheap velvet painting of a nude muscular man flexing. "What unique taste you have." I struggled to think of compliments. "I, um, love the sofa."

"Well, sit!" He took the cupcakes from me and set them on a cluttered coffee table, then pushed me back on the cushions. "I do most of my filming in here." Billy crossed the room to a closed wooden cabinet. He opened it, and the shelves were lined with dildos, fleshlights, and bottles of lube.

That was when I noticed a video camera directly across from me, with tungsten film lights folded up in a corner.

"You're in the industry?" I asked, and Billy nodded. "I'm assuming porn, right?"

"Of course." Billy giggled, then crossed the room and sat next to me. "I was on the coast filming my next feature, 'The Boys of Virginia Beach.'" He casually scooped up a bottle of poppers off the table, opened it, and sniffed. "Want some?"

"No, um, I really can't stay long with Jett across the hall." I needed to get out of there before Billy put the jam on me. His face was now red from the poppers, and a stupid grin stretched across his cheeks.

"If you ever need some extra cash, I'd love to work with you." Billy reached down and adjusted his package. "It's very simple work. You have to act like a straight guy down on his luck. Then you take your clothes off, lie back on the couch, and I get you off." He patted my thigh and I tried not to outwardly cringe. He was totally bizarre, but still a nice guy. "I can only use you once. It's an easy five hundred smackers, and I'd love to work with both you and your boyfriend."

"Well, that's quite an offer." I jumped up, grabbed the cupcakes, and hurried toward the door.

"Did I scare you off?" Billy leapt to his feet. "I didn't mean to. But you and your boyfriend are the best-looking guys I've ever had a chance to work with. Most of my guys are hustlers, or real dudes down on their luck." He raced over and placed his hands on my shoulders and licked his lips. "If the two of you appeared in a threeway with me, I'll double the cash."

Jesus, the money was tempting, but the thought of Billy touching me like that made me want to hurl. Plus, Jett would definitely be freaked out, considering he didn't even know what OnlyFans was. This was porn, and apparently he didn't watch much of it. "Billy, thanks for the offer, but my agent would drop me like a hot potato if I did something like that. She's already lining work up for me, and if it got out that I did porn, she'd totally flip out."

"Oh c'mon." He grabbed my elbow and pulled me back into the living room. "It's all tastefully done. See?" He grabbed a remote control off the coffee table, pushed a few buttons and a large screen came down from the ceiling. I needed to get out of there, but I had to admit, I was curious about his X-rated films. "This is the unedited footage I shot in Virginia. It's at a hotel on the banks of the Elizabeth river."

Billy's face filled the screen, then panned out and a rough, muscular-looking dude walked into the room. The sound was off, so I couldn't hear what they were saying. Then Billy dropped to his knees in front of the guy and began mouthing the dude's cock through his filthy jeans.

"His name is Leo, and he has the dick of death!" Billy giggled, then I felt his hand on my ass. I jumped away, then heard a male voice behind me.

"What the hell is going on in... oh my God."

We both spun around to see Jett with his mouth hanging open.

"Is this porn?" Jett pointed at the TV, and Billy leered at him. "Oh, that's you!"

"We've got to go." I bared my teeth at Billy, hoping it appeared friendly, though it felt strained and awkward. "See ya around, Billy."

————

"Okay, is everyone in LA as strange as that guy?" Jett fell back on the couch, pulled a white card out of his wallet, then started tapping on the screen of his phone.

"Hollywood is the dream factory, and some of those dreams are of the X-rated variety." I sat next to him and looked down at his phone. "Are you actually watching Billy's porno? Why?"

"I, um, I've never watched a lot of porn." Jett couldn't tear his eyes from the screen. "Porn always grossed me out. I don't like strangers touching me, so the thought of watching strangers having sex in a movie isn't appealing. Eww, look at this." He pointed at the screen. Billy was pulling the pants down on what appeared to be yet another hustler down on his luck. The guy had a cluster of bright red zits on his cheek, and when the pants were all the way off, I saw a few on his upper thighs.

"Do you really want to watch that?" I shivered. Personally, I liked sex, but preferred it with people I felt a connection with. "You know that's not real, right?"

Billy took the guy's cock in his hand and squeezed. The man's face brightened, and Billy's hand started traveling up and down the man's shaft.

"It looks real to me."

"I mean, yes, they're having sex, but it's not making love." It was the total opposite of making love. "Billy told me the deal. He pays them five hundred bucks to lie there while he gets them off. That's it. And for a guy down on his luck in Holly-wood, it's not bad money."

Jett turned to me, squinting his eyes. "He wanted you to act in one of these, didn't he? That's why he was showing you that movie."

Hm. Should I tell Jett that the offer was extended to him too?

"Yuck." Jett muttered. "There's no way I'd ever let that man touch me like that." He pointed at the screen. Billy was between the naked man's legs stuffing his cock down his throat. "You'd probably catch something you can't kill with a hammer."

I giggled, and Jett winked at me. Then we both turned our attention back to the phone. The man's head was laid against the back of the couch, and his eyes were shut. His hips were thrusting up and down while good old Billy deepthroated him. The guy moved his hands to the sides of Billy's head, urging him on.

"This is oddly fascinating." Jett murmured, and suddenly it dawned on me that I was with my ex-boyfriend watching porn. This had to be the oddest welcome to Hollyweird moment ever. "Like, they look like they're really getting into it."

The dude on the couch slapped Billy, who let the cock pop out of his mouth and smiled up at the guy. Spit covered his lower face, and his dark eyes appeared joyous, like he was having a religious experience. He resumed blowing the guy, and Jett shifted on the cushion next to me, his gaze intensifying.

Oh my God, was Jett getting turned on by this?

My cock twitched, and I realized I was getting turned on by watching Jett getting worked up. Jett hasn't even been here a single day and I was already perving on him. And after his experience with good 'ol Billy, I'd scare him to death if I even breathed on him the wrong way.

"I'm uh, thirsty." I stood up, then hurried to the kitchen. My dick was misbehaving, and hopefully it would deflate before I returned to the living room. I opened the refrigerator and pulled out the water pitcher. My hands trembled as I poured a glass, all the while counting from a thousand backwards to get rid of the boner. After downing the water, I crept to the doorway and peered into the living room.

Jett's eyes were still focused on the screen, and his neck was suspiciously pink. Was he actually turned on by Billy and that guy? His hand went down to his crotch and adjusted his junk.

It couldn't be Billy. No, that was impossible.

I must have made a noise because Jett's head jerked back, and his gaze locked with mine for a second.

"I'm uh, really exhausted." Jett started to get up, then he sat back down again, his face now matching his neck. Shit, now I was making him uncomfortable watching him. This had to end now.

"It's been a long day." I fake yawned, stretching my arms over my head. "I'm going to bed early. Help yourself to anything in the fridge, and tomorrow I'll show you around town." I hurried toward my bedroom, giving Jett a chance to leave the living room with his respect still intact.

When I got there I shut the door and sat on the edge of the bed. "I understand why I was turned on by Jett." I hit my pillow and fell back on the mattress. "But why on earth was he turned on by Billy and that guy?"

CHAPTER 7

JETT

The last few days felt like an awkward dream—you know, the ones where you were standing in front of a class and realized you were naked? No matter how you tried to cover yourself, everyone pointed and laughed.

Our neighbor, Billy, really opened my eyes to the bizarre side of Hollywood, but even worse was my attraction to Chris. When we sat there on the sofa looking at porn together (awkward!), all I could imagine was doing what I saw on my phone's screen with Chris. I sensed I might've freaked him out, and when I crawled under the blankets to jerk one out, I realized Chris might think I was turned on by Billy's video.

Yuck.

Needless to say, whenever the topic of our pervy neighbor came up, I changed the subject.

Aside from that bizarre encounter, things were looking up. For the first time ever, I hit over a hundred thousand streams on the various music streaming sites, bringing in a little more than three grand. Add to that, merchandise sales and physical sales of my work, and I made just a hair under 4K. It sounded like a decent amount of money until you factored in taxes and production costs. That wiped out almost half of the cash, so I decided to get a part-time job waiting tables. This was my one chance to hit the big time, and I wasn't about to fuck it up by going broke.

Today was my first day as a pseudo-cowboy waiter at this gay bar Chris liked called Flaming Saddles. He said I'd make tons of cash, though the way he said it made me feel awkward. Jesus, everything made me feel awkward. Chris claimed that with my looks, I'd make a killing. I nearly laughed in his face when he said it.

"This place is nothing like Virginia." I picked up my new work uniform, turned it around, and realized the chaps didn't have an ass. "Oh fuck, there's no way I can wear this." I tossed the outfit back in the plastic bag it came in, then saw several pairs of hot pink thongs. A note was attached to one of them.

It's a requirement for all waitstaff to wear the thongs under the chaps to avoid breaking Los Angeles County regulations.

"Well, we wouldn't want to do that."

————

I really wasn't sure what to expect as I walked into Flaming Saddles for my first day of training. The place was packed and the music was loud, but my eyes were immediately drawn to the huge man behind the bar. He had a thick black beard, an impressive set of tattoos, and a colorful shirt with the words "Gabe" stitched onto it. He caught me looking at him and winked at me.

"You're lucky I'm training you instead of Gabe." A guy grabbed my arm and steered me to the rear of the bar. He pushed open a set of double doors, then walked me through a busy kitchen. There was a door by the large freezers. He opened it and gestured for me to enter.

"Why am I lucky?" I asked, gazing around the small locker room.

"Because he's a dick who will demand almost all of your tips in exchange for his help. My name is Cam, and for the next week I'll teach you the ins and outs of waiting tables in Hollywood's largest gay cowboy bar."

Cam opened a locker and handed me a slip of paper. "That's the combination. Keep your street clothes in here. Oh, and don't leave valuables in there. Some of the other servers have sticky fingers and serious lock-picking skills." Cam grinned a blinding white smile. Jesus, every single person I'd met so far in Hollyweird had seriously perfect teeth. He was probably an actor or model on the side.

"So, what brings you to LA?" Cam asked. "Are you trying to break into show business like everyone else?" He opened a locker and stripped off his shirt.

"How could you tell I'm new to town?" I opened the bag with the uniform and felt embarrassed to put it on.

"Nobody is from Hollywood, and you've got those deer caught in headlights look that all new arrivals have." Cam laughed, then sat on the low wooden bench in front of the lockers and toed off his sneakers.

Shit, I can't believe I'm about to put on a pair of assless chaps with a neon pink thong. "Um, I'm a musician, and I was hoping..."

"Hey," Cam tilted his head and pointed at me. "You look familiar." He stood up and peeled his jeans off. I turned away, since he didn't have anything underneath them. "Your name is Jett Sumner. Aren't you the guy who sings that song *Take Me At Face Value?*"

"Woah, you know my music?" I was surprised. "Yeah, that's

me But how did you know that?" I heard his locker open, then I snuck a glance and saw him sliding the pink thong up his legs.

"I recognized your name and I love your music, dude. I'm also in the industry, and I keep tabs on who's who around here," he said, and I detected a smirk in his voice. "My other job is at The Scorpio Room, booking talent. We stream your music a lot there. Why on earth are you waiting tables? I hear your music all the time."

I barely heard what he said because I was forcing myself to pull down my jeans and get completely naked in front of a stranger. Once my jeans and underwear were off I hurriedly pulled on the tacky thong and slid the chaps up my legs.

"Well, I'm seeing some success, but until a few days ago I lived in Virginia, which isn't the optimal place to build a music career. So I moved here, and I took this job to make sure I have steady money while taking the next step." I pulled the t-shirt over my head, then felt dressed enough to face Cam again.

He crossed his arms over his chest and cocked an eyebrow at me.

"Well, then you'd better get used to working hard if you want to make it big out here," Cam said with a wink."I might be able to book you at The Scorpio Room. Who's your agent?"

"Um, I'm still working on that." My face turned red, and Cam gestured toward the door.

"You write great tunes, dude, and you've got that whole Harry Styles thing with your looks. When you find an agent, and you will, let me know and maybe I can help you out. But let's get you trained first on how things work here at Flaming Saddles."

I opened the door, and when Cam strolled through it, he said over his shoulder, "Always remember: no matter how long

THE BIG TIME   45

your shift is or how tired you are... never leave your money unattended."

———

As I nervously followed Cam throughout Flaming Saddles, I was struck by the sheer size of the place. The room was huge, with shiny wood paneling and chandeliers made out of deer antlers. Neon beer signs dotted the walls, and there was a dance floor the size of a basketball court in the center of the bar.

Cam's voice broke through my thoughts, pulling me back to reality. "This is where you'll be spending your night," he said, gesturing toward a section of the bar near the pool tables, pinball machines, and a mechanical bull. "It's the slowest section of the bar, but don't worry, you'll still make decent cash."

Cam spent the next hour showing me how to use the register and place orders at the bar. Then he took the section next to mine so he could make money, too.

Things went great for the next couple of hours, and the wad of cash in my pocket grew with every tip. Then there was a commotion toward the front of the bar.

Cam and I were at the waiters' station when it happened, and we craned our heads to see what was going on.

"Holy shit, is that Hugo Zapeda and Becket Grant?" He pointed at a small group of people walking through the crowd. A moment later they strolled into my section with Chris and a woman I hadn't met in tow.

"Hey man, I wanted to introduce you to Hugo, Becket, and my agent, Marla." Chris gave me a brief bro hug. "Marla is Hugo's sister."

I glanced over to Cam, who's eyes were like saucers.

"I've heard great things about you." Marla said, shaking my

hand. "According to Chris, you're the next big thing in pop music."

"Um, thanks." I led them to a table, and when I turned around to get their menus, I realized almost everyone in the bar was trying to stare at them without looking obvious. Turning back to them, I muttered, "Sorry about them." I waved my hand toward the people staring. Even though I was a fan of Hugo and Becket, I'd heard all about them from Chris, which kept me from being too starstruck.

Hugo smiled and wrapped an arm around Becket's shoulder. "It feels great being around real people for a change."

Becket pecked Hugo on the cheek, and I heard several guys around us gasp. "Coming out of the closet was the best thing I ever did," he added quietly.

"So, what can I get you guys to drink?" I asked, and after I took their orders I raced to the register to send it to the bar where I would pick it up.

Cam threw his arm over my shoulder and whispered, "Jesus, you don't need my help getting ahead in this business. How the hell do you know them?"

I shrugged, then hurried to the bar to fetch their drinks. When I returned, Marla began speaking as I placed their drinks down in front of them.

"Chris played me your music, and I did a little social media sleuthing. You've got quite a following on both TikTok and Instagram." She picked up her gin and tonic and sipped it. "I want to be your agent, but I have to be honest with you upfront. The music business is a mystery to me, but I have contacts in every other part of the industry, and if you trust me, I will make you a star."

I stared at Marla, dumbstruck. Not only was she offering to be my agent, but she had also done her research and knew what I was capable of. I glanced around the bar again, feeling like I must be dreaming. Then I felt Chris's hand on top of mine. His green eyes sparkled, and a slow smile spread across his face.

"I told you, Jett. You've got real talent. All I did was point Marla in your direction." He removed his hand, and I was tempted to snatch it back. I couldn't believe he went to bat for me, and so quickly too.

Marla smiled, then pushed a lock of wavy burgundy hair behind her ear. "You have something special, and I can help make your dreams a reality. Plus I'm expanding my client base and want to enter the music scene. Think of it this way. You'll be helping me, and I'll help you in return."

Shit. Why did this have to happen while I was at work? I felt overwhelmed, though I wasn't about to turn her down.

"Thank you," I sputtered. "It's a deal. But why me?"

CHAPTER 8

CHRIS

"This never happens." I yawned, then sat up in bed. My alarm was set to go off in fifteen minutes, so I turned it off. For the first time in a long time I had three excellent reasons to wake up early.

First, I was meeting with a photographer who was shooting catalog shots for Neiman Marcus. This was an ongoing assignment, so today they were taking measurements for clothes and headshots. Marla lived up to her word, and the Neiman Marcus gig ensured I had a steady paycheck for the immediate future.

Second and third, I had two auditions. The first was for the Shop From Home Network, where I was hoping to become a presenter. The second audition was for a guest star slot on a television show about teen angels. According to the script I was playing a demon sent from hell to torture innocent nuns at a haunted convent.

I swung my feet over the side of the bed and winced when my feet hit the cold floor. After padding into the bathroom I nearly scared myself when I saw my reflection in the mirror.

"Fucking palm trees." My nose was running, eyes were

puffy and bloodshot, and my lips were ragged from the dry air. I loved California, but when I moved here I had no idea I was allergic to palm trees. The orange dust was toxic as far as I was concerned, so I took two antihistamines and raced to the kitchen.

I kept two metal spoons in the freezer for days like this. After sitting on a stool I placed the cold spoons against my closed eyelids and waited for them to do their magic.

"Morning," Jett's voice sounded as tired as my eyes. "What are you doing?"

I removed one of the spoons so I could look at him. Nice. All he was wearing was a red t-shirt and black pajama bottoms.

"The cold spoons take down puffiness." I put the spoon back against my eye. "I have a modeling gig this morning, and I woke up looking like hell. It's the damned palm trees. I hope you don't have allergies too."

I felt a slight breeze as Jett walked past me, then heard the freezer open.

"No problems with allergies, but since I've never been around palm trees before, who knows." Jett mumbled, then the smell of coffee beans filled the air. "Should I make enough coffee for both of us?"

"No coffee before a photo shoot. Can't hold a pose if I'm jittery." I removed the spoons, and nearly jumped in my seat. Jett was a foot away from me, his eyes glued to my face. He jumped back, his face flushing.

"Oh, sorry." Jett turned and began filling the coffee pot with water.

"I'd stick around for breakfast, but I can't be late." I stood, then Jett cleared his throat.

"Are you going to be around later?" He asked, his fingers fumbling with the buttons on the coffee maker.

"Sure," I replied. "Now that I've got money coming in, maybe I can take us out for a drink."

———

The photo shoot went well, but I knew how to do it. Don't outshine the clothes, just be a human clothes hanger. But now that I was auditioning for more acting roles, I felt lost at sea. And this first audition wasn't even acting. I was supposed to be a presenter on one of those tacky shopping networks.

Everyone waiting for their audition was seriously dressed up. The women all looked like drag queens, with puffy blonde hair and inch-thick makeup. The guys were all middle-aged, wearing boring suits, and several had thick makeup on too. Me, I was dressed in a pair of khaki slacks and an Armani t-shirt Hugo gave me for my last birthday.

"Oh, thank God I caught you!" I glanced up while Marla sat in the beige plastic chair next to me. "I think I made a big mistake booking you for this audition." She grimaced. "Tell me something. Do you know how to be a presenter?"

My heart raced as I shook my head, but Marla patted my arm reassuringly. "It'll be okay," she said. "Just talk about the product, keep it light and fun, and don't forget to smile." She quickly typed something into her phone. "I want to talk to you about something after your audition, so I'll wait for you."

"Chris Reynolds?" A man with thick black glasses and a dorky haircut stood in the doorway of the waiting room. "You're next."

I glanced at Marla, who had a strand of hair in her mouth. She spat it out and muttered, "Break a leg."

I'd never auditioned for being a presenter before, and I had no idea what they expected from me, so I just concentrated on keeping a pleasant smile on my face as I waited for them to begin speaking.

There were two women, both resembling beauty queens from the 1980s, and a bored-looking man seated behind a piano. An enormous plush banana toy was leaning against the wall behind the piano, looking wildly out of place.

"Chris, my name is Chastity Parrish, and I'm the hostess of our children's segment where we sell everything from infant wear to video games for young teens." She grinned the usual Hollywood smile of blinding white teeth. They probably cost what I made last year. "This is Betty Lynn, our executive producer." A woman wearing a green satin dress with massive shoulder pads yawned. "And that's Paul Cramer. He's accompanying you on the piano today."

What the actual fuck?

"You want me to sing?" I muttered, and Chastity's smile turned upside down.

"Well, yes. We're trying something new, adding music to our presentations. Didn't you know that before the audition?" She glanced over to Betty Lynn, who was pulling a compact out of a large purse.

Damn it, why hadn't Marla told me there was going to be singing? I could barely sing karaoke. How was I supposed to pull off this audition without making a fool of myself?

The seconds ticked by in agonizing slow motion as I stood there, trying to think of something witty or clever to say that would save me from this horrible situation.

But before I could even form a sentence, Chastity handed me the sheet music and said, "Let's hear what you've got. Oh, and if you could dance too, I'd appreciate it."

I glanced down at the paper, unable to understand the scribbles. Then I saw the lyrics and prayed my face didn't give away my horror.

"It's in the key of C." The pianist drawled, then he began playing. Shit. A moment later, he stopped. "You missed your cue."

"This guy has the looks we want." The producer tossed back her hair. "Once more from the top."

Okay. I've got the look, so let's pray they overlook my lack of singing ability. Oh, and dancing too. The pianist began again, and this time I opened my mouth and began singing the silly children's song while bouncing up and down.

I've got a pet banana, he's yellow and round

He loves to sing and dance when there's no one around

He wears a little hat and a pair of red shoes

And every time he sings, he makes the whole room shake loose

Chastity rolled her eyes, but I decided to keep going.

Banana, banana, silly little guy

He's always making me laugh, no matter how hard I try

Banana, banana, with a smile so wide

He's my best friend, and he's always by my side.

The pianist stopped playing, and Chastity and Betty Lynn eyed each other.

"Thank you for auditioning today." Chastity muttered. "Next."

———

"I swear they didn't mention anything about singing." Marla tapped on her phone and handed it to me. "Read the email."

We were walking down a long beige corridor toward the parking lot. Since I'd taken an Uber here, she was giving me a lift to my next audition. I glanced over the email, and she was right. I'd been ambushed by the fucking banana song.

"It was awful, Marla." I handed her the phone back. "I had to sing and dance to this stupid song about a pet banana, and..."

"Sweetie, I hate to tell you this, but this kind of crap happens all the time." We got to the exit and she held the door open for me. "And remember, every audition you go on, the better you'll become. This is why I want you to take an acting class. They'll teach you how to maximize each audition. Trust me, Chris, I wouldn't have signed you on as a client if I didn't believe in you."

"If only I believed in me too."

———

I kicked off my shoes as soon as I got home. All I wanted to do was drink a beer and lose myself in stupid reality shows, but beer was off limits since I had an early morning photo shoot. Both auditions had gone terribly, and I was beginning to think that maybe I should accept the fact that acting just wasn't for me. After all, what did I know how to do besides stand there and look pretty?

But then Marla's words came back to me: "Every audition you go on, the better you'll become." She believed in me, so why shouldn't I believe in myself?

"From her lips to God's ears." I shook my head and padded down the hall to my bedroom so I could change into something more comfortable.

When I walked past Jett's room, I stopped and pressed my ear against his door, wondering if he was home. I liked having him here, and wanted someone to commiserate with. Not hearing anything, I continued on to my room.

"I want more than posing in front of a camera." I sighed, sat on the edge of my bed, and kicked off my loafers. "Like, I want to make something of myself."

I pulled my t-shirt over my head and tossed it to the floor. Hugo wins awards, goes to premiers, and appears in all the important magazines. Why can't I have that too? I stood up, pulled my pants off and kicked them next to the abandoned t-shirt.

"Oh, shit."

I glanced up to see Jett spinning around. Why, I didn't know since we'd seen each other naked before, and I still had my boxer briefs on.

"It's okay dude." I giggled, then raced into my closet and put on a pair of cut-off jeans and a holey black t-shirt. "I'm glad you're here. Today was hellish."

Jett bit his lower lip, and my memory kicked into overdrive. The very first guy I kissed was beet red, and staring at the floor. Jesus, Jett was a shy one. I didn't remember him being so skittish when we'd briefly dated all those years ago.

"I wasn't going to drink beer tonight, but what the hell. After the day I had, you want to join me?" I closed the distance between us, and Jett muttered, "Sure."

We walked into the kitchen together, not saying a word. I grabbed two beers from the fridge, and when I handed him one our fingers briefly touched. Jett's brown eyes met mine for a moment, and that sexy blush reddened his cheeks.

"I want you to listen to a demo of a song I started writing today." Jett turned and I followed him down the hallway to his bedroom. He'd set up his keyboards, and an acoustic guitar lay on the bed next to a set of headphones. That's why I didn't hear anything when I eavesdropped on him. "Sit." He gestured toward the bed, and I sat on the edge of it. He sat on the floor at my feet where his laptop was.

"I wish I was musical." I ran a finger over the guitar strings. "I had to sing at an audition today. It was horrific."

Jett laughed, then typed something into his laptop. A moment later a steady beat came from two tiny speakers perched on the dresser drawers. This sounded different from his other stuff, more electronic. Then his voice came through the speakers, and for a moment I forgot where I was.

I didn't know music well, but I loved Jett's voice. It went from high notes to low ones without a hitch, and it had a masculine timbre that sent chills up my spine. I didn't even pay attention to the lyrics, just let the beats and his voice wash through me. Jett was passionate about something, and whatever it was, it sounded sexy as hell.

The song ended and Jett looked up at me with a shy smile. I couldn't help but grin back at him. He seemed pleased with my reaction.

"What did you think?" he asked, dipping his head down.

"It was amazing," I replied without hesitation. "You're going to be a huge star, Jett. I feel it in my bones."

Jett sighed, placed his laptop back on the floor, and lay down next to it.

"It's official." Jett stretched his arms over his head and yawned, pulling his t-shirt up over his belly button. Suddenly I couldn't see anything else but the brown hairs of his happy trail, snaking into his shorts. "I signed with Marla today."

"I'm sorry, what did you say?" I stuttered, and forced myself to stare out the window.

"Marla is now my agent." Jett stared up at the ceiling.

Marla hadn't said a word about it to me. "That's great news, right?" Jett didn't sound very enthusiastic.

"Yes, but I'm not sure I want to follow all of her advice." He sat up, and I allowed my gaze to meet his. "She wants me to make more electronic music, you know, club stuff. Plus, she wants me to take dance lessons."

"Is that a bad thing?" I asked. Hell, that was mostly the type of music I listened to.

"Well, she says that's where my audience is. Gay guys

mostly sing dance pop. The problem is, I have two left feet." He sat up and crossed his arms over his knees.

"Oh dude, I know exactly how you feel." I laughed. "Marla sent me to an audition today as a presenter on a home shopping network. She says she didn't know in advance, but I had to sing a stupid kid song about bananas." I laughed, finally allowing the absurdity of that audition to sink in. "I can't sing to save my life. But the thing is, I think Marla is getting a feel for what we are capable of. She's been very successful representing Hugo, so I think we should both give her a chance."

"I get it, and I'm grateful for the opportunities she swears I'll get with her by my side." Jett stood, grabbed his beer off the dresser and took a long swig. A foamy mustache covered his upper lip. "But I'm afraid of losing who I am trying to be more commercial."

It suddenly struck me what Jett's appeal was. Not only did he have the talent, and most definitely the looks, but he was innocent. A dreamer, unprepared for Hollywood and the compromises we had to make to earn a living here.

"Jett, trust me when I say this, but I believe in you, and so does Marla." I stood and placed an arm over his shoulder. He stiffened, and I suddenly felt uncomfortable. I backed away from him and looked him dead in the eye.

"Jett, the question is, do you believe in yourself?"

CHAPTER 9

JETT

Chris's words echoed in my head when I fell asleep last night, and I couldn't stop thinking about them.

"Believe in yourself."

The idea of becoming a pop star seemed far-fetched, but I had to admit it was what I wanted. I yearned to be successful, to be recognized and respected by my peers. But even more than that, I wanted all the money.

Did I have the guts to go after what I craved? Did I have the discipline to make it happen? Could I make the sacrifices necessary to reach the top?

"I believe in myself, or I never would've come to Hollywood." I sighed, then eyed my work uniform at the foot of the bed. Waiting tables sucked, but I had to admit the money was decent. The worst part was the uniform, and having to get naked in front of my coworkers. I even thought about wearing the uniform to the bar. But since I walked to work, the thought of strangers seeing me in the hot pink thong and assless chaps made my blood run cold.

"Fuck it," I stood up and grabbed the thong. "I'll just wear it under my jeans. At least I won't have to get completely naked."

It was strange, this shyness I never realized I had. For God's sake, I loved getting on stage and performing in front of crowds of people, and my usual stage costume was as campy as you could get. But it felt creepy getting naked in the tiny locker room in the back of Flaming Saddles.

I pulled my shorts off, removed my boxers and pulled the tiny scrap of pink fabric up my legs. When I was onstage, I typically wore a bright-red sequined jumpsuit with flared trousers and a shimmering cape, usually paired with scruffy combat boots. But my waiter's uniform made me feel like a perv. Actually, that was wrong. It made me feel exposed, like all the Billy's in the world could ogle me.

My bedroom door opened, and my hands went down to cover my junk. "Hey, you got a… sorry, Jett!"

Chris stood there staring at me in the hideous pink thong, and suddenly I realized how ridiculous I looked. Fuck being embarrassed, I should own it.

"The shit we do for money." I winked, then grabbed my jeans and slid them on. When I buttoned the top button, I glanced at Chris, and I'd swear he was stoned, or his pupils were dilated for some reason.

He licked his lips, then spoke, "Yeah, I model underwear sometimes, and it's always awkward."

Speaking of awkward, Chris watching me get dressed was definitely uncomfortable. But it wasn't like he hadn't seen me naked before. I felt my cheeks burn at the memory. "So, what did you want?"

"Um, shit I forgot." Chris giggled, and I noticed his eyes dropping to the floor. "Sorry. I'd better um, leave you to it."

Before I could say another word, the door shut behind him.

I glanced down at my phone. "Damn it, it's only eight o'clock."

My pockets were almost empty, holding just fourteen dollars in tips that I'd scraped together since the start of my shift. Remembering that I was the new guy, I hesitantly approached the husky bearded bartender who was in charge to ask if he would let me leave early.

"Gabe," I shuffled up to him. "It's dead tonight and it doesn't seem like things are going to pick up anytime soon. Do you think it would be okay if I head out early?"

He raised his eyebrows and leaned against the counter for a moment, contemplating my request. "Dude, it's Wednesday night — this place usually starts hopping around nine. You sure you want to cut out now?"

God, I really did. But, until I was on firmer footing with my music career, it was best that I stay put. "Forget I asked. Hopefully it'll get busy soon."

"Attaboy," Gabe winked, and went back to cleaning glasses.

"Well, well, well." A familiar voice rang out behind me. "I'd swear my neighbors have been avoiding me." I slowly turned around and immediately blushed. It was Billy Higgins from across the hall, with two guys my age who looked like they'd been put through the wringer. Tonight he was wearing a navy-blue velour tracksuit, and a stack of gold necklaces were draped around his crepey neck. How the older man constantly had dates with younger guys baffled me.

Oh yeah. He paid for them.

"Hey, Billy." I grinned, forcing myself not to think about what he had already done with them, or what he was about to do. "Been busy. Got a part-time gig here, and working on my music every chance I get."

"Where's your section?" Billy put his arm over my shoulder, and I prayed he didn't have anything contagious.

"Over there, by the mechanical bull." I pointed to the rear of the bar and Billy handed me a twenty dollar bill. "Get us each a beer, and we'll meet you over there." Billy smacked one of the dudes' ass, and they strolled to the back of the bar and sat down.

For a moment I stood there, watching the three of them laugh about something. Jesus, I never knew what a prude I was until I moved to LA. It seemed like everyone here was open to anything x-rated. Living in Richmond, I never even thought about pervy stuff. Not that I was a virgin or anything. I'd been with a handful of guys, and except for Chris, none of them had been serious. They were more like a way of passing the time until I got my big break. And the only reason I'd say it was serious with Chris is because he was my first. Well, my first kiss, and my first boyfriend. We were young back then, and things never progressed very far in the bedroom. Mostly we fooled around in the backseat of his car. It was difficult when both of us were living with our parents.

"Are you going to place their orders or not?" Gabe barked, and when I turned to him I blushed. I did an awful lot of that here. He slid three pint glasses across the bar. "I know what Billy drinks. How do you know him?" Gabe waggled his thick brows. "Is it the way most of us know him?"

Oh. My. God.

Did he actually think I'd been in one of Billy's porno videos?

"Um, if you are referring to his..."

"Dude, it's the easiest five hundred bucks you'll ever make. All you do is lie back, and he makes you..."

"No, and I'm not interested." I placed the beers on my tray and hurried to Billy's table. Jesus, I wondered how many of my coworkers had been in porn? And Gabe? That just struck me as weird. He was a burly bear, not some down on his luck twink. Then again, I had a feeling Good 'ol Billy would do it with anyone possessing a working penis.

"Gage, Tommy, this is my neighbor from across the hall, Jett." Billy sipped his beer. "I keep trying to get him to make a little movie with me, but no bueno."

The guys shrugged and downed half their beers at once. They were both tall, broad-shouldered, and had tattoos crawling up their necks.

"Nice to meet you," I replied, realizing they probably didn't give a fuck if I said anything or not. Billy put his arm over my shoulders, and my nose filled with the scent of his overpowering aftershave. I felt his hand on my ass, and nearly screamed. Thankfully, two normal looking pseudo-cowboys sat down in my section.

"Gotta go, Billy." I stepped away from the table. "I'll come back and check on you in a little bit."

If there is a God, please send a crowd of guys in here now. If I had to entertain the old perv and his so-called actors for long, I'd lose my mind.

———

"Thanks," I shut the door to the Uber and hurried inside the apartment building. Instead of walking I called a driver. Soon after Billy and his friends arrived at the bar, it became nuts. After tipping out the bartenders I had almost three hundred bucks in my pockets and didn't feel safe walking alone.

It was almost two in the morning, so I was trying to be as quiet as possible. When the door to the apartment opened, it was dark inside. I flipped on the lights and tiptoed to the kitchen. I was starving, and hoped there was a leftover slice of pizza in the fridge.

"Hey Jett."

"Jesus Christ!" I jumped, clutching my chest. I spun around, and Chris leaned against the wall on the opposite side of the kitchen. My eyes widened at the sight. Damn, the pics he posted on social media didn't do him justice. He was wearing nothing but a pair of gray sweatpants cut off mid-thigh. His abs rippled down his stomach and led to what could only be described as a package worth drooling over.

"What are you doing here?" I asked, trying to keep my voice steady despite my racing heart.

"I live here." Chris smirked. "Busy night at the bar?" He yawned, then reached down and adjusted his junk.

"Um, yeah." I opened the fridge and pulled out the greasy cardboard box of pizza and set it on the counter. "Very busy. I'm starving." I opened it and pulled out a slice.

Chris crossed the room and snagged a slice too. "Hope you don't mind, but I forgot to eat dinner." He looked into my eyes with an intensity normally not reserved for leftover pizza. Chris brought the slice to his mouth and bit into it, his eyes not leaving mine. Suddenly it felt like I couldn't breathe. My eyes dropped, and I'd swear there was a large banana swinging around underneath his gray sweats. I blushed, and lifted my gaze back to Chris's face. The hand holding the slice of pizza was frozen in front of his face, a knowing smile stretched across his cheeks.

Damn it, he caught me staring at his bulge.

"I'm really, um, tired." I backed out of the kitchen, wanting to hide, but wanting to stay too. Once I reached the hallway I hurried to my bedroom. After shutting the door closed I placed the slice of pizza on the dresser, no longer hungry. Well, not hungry for pizza. I stripped off my jeans, and tore the flimsy pink thong off in my haste to get naked. Then I climbed under the covers, grabbed my dick and whispered, "This is the last time." I squeezed it, and a whimper came out of my throat. "No more fantasizing about Chris."

With my other hand I pressed on the skin under my balls, then another thought passed through my head.

"What if he was wearing those flimsy shorts on purpose?"

CHAPTER 10
CHRIS

t worked.

I knew the chemistry we shared as teenagers still existed, but last night confirmed it.

Even though I had to wake up early for work, I set my alarm for one in the morning. After crawling out of bed I slid on a pair of cut-off gray sweats, then I waited for Jett to come home. I might be exhausted now, but the look on Jett's face when I strolled into the kitchen was worth it.

The air felt electric last night, and if I closed my eyes I could picture Jett spinning around, eyes wide at the sight of me. His gaze was like a caress, his eyes taking in my body and coming to a stop on my face. We might not have seen each other in years, but what was that old saying? *Absence makes the heart grow fonder.* Or was it, *absence makes the dick grow harder*? Whatever it was, the chemistry between us had only grown stronger.

I wish I'd been brave enough to take things to the next level, but I chickened out. I should've taken his hand, yes, that was what I should have done. Jett was a romantic who loved nothing more than midnight walks in the park, or talking all night in a coffee shop about our dreams of the future. At least that was how he used to be.

He wants me, and now I know it. So what's the next step?

———

"Do you like my new office?" Marla asked, and I had to admit I was impressed. The room was modern with sleek furniture, a wooden desk that could double as a bar, and an impressive view of the Hollywood sign. Apparently she was making money now that Hugo's career had taken off. Now I wanted a piece of the action, too.

"It beats the hell out of your living room," I laughed. Marla winked, then gestured for me to sit in the chrome and leather chair in front of her desk. "So what's this meeting about?"

Marla inhaled, then steepled her fingers under her chin. "I spoke with the casting director from your last audition, and from what she said, we have work to do."

I shifted uneasily in my chair, feeling like I was about to be scolded. "I know it wasn't my best performance," I began, trying to sound confident.

Marla nodded. "It's not that you weren't good, it's just that your skills weren't polished enough for the part. You need to learn the basics of acting and get some practice." She paused for a moment before continuing. "So here's what I suggest. I've already tracked down three great acting classes taught by one of the best schools in Los Angeles."

The thought of taking an acting class filled me with excitement and dread at the same time. On the one hand, I wanted to work on my craft and become better suited for roles like the one I lost out on; but on the other hand, being put under a microscope by a teacher made me feel like a teenager again.

"I think it's worth a shot," Marla said encouragingly as she pulled out a brochure from her desk drawer and handed it to me. "Take your time and consider all of your options."

My heart raced as I looked over the brochure and read about the stellar reputation of this particular school. The Hollywood Acting Academy.

"Look, if you really want to make it in this business you've got to make some sacrifices – like humbling yourself enough to accept criticism from the best teachers in LA." Marla grinned. "Honestly, Chris, you've got the looks to go far, but unfortunately, this is a cutthroat industry. You must become more than a pretty face, and acting classes will help."

"Okay," I drew the word out. "How much does it cost, because I'm..."

"Give me a second." Marla tapped on the keyboard of her desktop computer. "You have almost forty-five-grand worth of modeling bookings for the next six months. So acting..."

"What?" I gasped. "You've got to be kidding me. I didn't even make that much last year." Jesus, Marla was a much better agent than that old man.

"As I was saying, you can afford a class or three." Marla tapped on the keyboard again. "Chris, you're a natural in front of the camera, so that's not a problem. It's more about honing your skills as an actor, so your performances feel more natural. Open the brochure, please."

I did as she asked, and the list of classes was overwhelming. Was I really so bad I had to...

"I think you only need three classes. The audition technique class, the cold reading class, and a method acting class." Marla stood and went to the bar on the other side of her office. "Want something to drink?"

"Water's great." I replied. "What's the cold reading class about?"

Marla placed a bottle of mineral water on the desk in front

of me and sat down. "It's super important. So, the casting director's primary complaint was that you couldn't understand the material at a glance. Cold reading is when you must perform at a moment's notice using a script you're unfamiliar with."

"Uh huh." I shrugged, not understanding what she meant.

"For example, I hand you the script for Teen Angels. You have no idea what the story is about, but if you excel at cold reading, you can figure that shit out, fast." Marla tapped her manicured nails on the desk. "The audition technique class is similar, but that focuses more on helping you stand out from all the other actors auditioning. The combination of the..." The phone on her desk buzzed. She tapped a button and her new receptionist's voice came through the intercom.

"Ms. Fleming, Ram Khapoor called to say he's running ten minutes late for his appointment with you. Is that going to be okay?"

"No problem, he's my last appointment of the day and I don't mind staying late for him." She disconnected the call. "Do you know Ram? He's a friend of Becket's."

"I've met him once or twice."

"He's a huge star in Bollywood, but the real money is here in LA. I'm hoping to sign him as a client." She grinned and got to her feet. "Since I know your modeling schedule, I'm signing you up for the classes that will work with it. The fees are in the brochure I gave you, and I'll subtract them from your pay so you don't have to worry about it." She walked around the desk and hugged me. "You're going to be a star, Chris. Just put in the work, and I promise you'll be a success." She let go of me, then placed her hands on my shoulders, locking her gaze with mine. "One more thing. I need you to spend more time with Hugo and Becket, and post pics of you guys on social media. They both know about it, so just give them a ring and go to a restaurant or bar. Oh, and make Jett come along for those too. The publicity is worth its weight in gold." She let go of me and walked me to the door. "And tell Jett I have excellent news for him, but I have to finalize the details first."

———

I decided to take a walk down by the Santa Monica pier. It had been awhile since I had taken some time off to just relax and enjoy the beach. The sun was setting, and the beach was quiet. It felt like a world away from the chaos and stress of Hollyweird.

The sound of the waves lapping against the shore calmed my nerves, and I sat on a bench near the edge of the water and just watched. The sky was painted in hues of pink, orange, yellow, and blue as the sun slowly sank into the horizon. It was so peaceful and calming that I almost forgot about all of my problems for a moment. Then I noticed a familiar face, some reality television star taking selfies a few yards away. That was enough to wreck the moment.

"Time to go home." I sighed, then I picked up my shoes and started walking back toward the boardwalk. Once there I put my shoes back on and called an Uber.

"So what am I going to do about Jett?" I muttered. Despite work, and my meeting with Marla, I couldn't get Jett out of my head. Normally, I didn't want more than sex, and despite the easy availability of men in Hollywood, I didn't sleep around much. But this connection with Jett went deeper, and I wondered if he felt the same.

"There's only one way to find out."

———

As soon as I opened the front door I heard Jett strumming his guitar in his bedroom. For a moment, I just stood there listening, feeling the music wash through me. It was beautiful and captivating. I realized that even if things didn't work out with Jett, I'd always want us to at least be friends.

"Fuck that," I whispered. I wanted more, and if last night was any indication, so did he.

I kicked off my shoes then tiptoed down the hallway to his room. When I lifted my hand to knock on his door, I froze.

"C'mon." I muttered under my breath. Taking a deep breath, I moved my hand forward, and his door flew open.

"Oh my God!" We said at the same time, and a huge grin split Jett's face. We just stood there for a moment, taking each other in.

"Hi," he finally said, his voice low and husky.

"Hi," I replied, my heart pounding. "I've been thinking about you all day."

CHAPTER 11

JETT

"You have?" My knees trembled, but I was determined not to let fear stop me from seeing if the attraction I felt for Chris was mutual. I wanted to close the distance between us, and feel his lips pressed against mine.

"Yes, Jett." Chris took a step closer. "You've been on my mind a lot lately."

There was a moment of silence as I processed what Chris had said. I'd been on his mind? That could only mean one thing; he felt the same way about me. It felt like I was standing on the edge of a cliff, my feet trembling, unsure of what would happen if I took the plunge.

I stepped closer to Chris, the gap between us narrowing until I could feel the heat radiating from his body. His eyes were hazy with emotion, and I could feel my heart pounding in my chest.

In a moment of boldness, I reached up and cupped his face in my hands. I could feel his stubble against my palms, and I wanted to run my hands down his chest.

"Are you sure this is what you want?" Chris murmured, and I closed my eyes, pulling him towards me until our lips met.

The kiss was gentle and electric, like a jolt of energy coursing through my veins. Chris's hands were on my waist and I felt myself melting into him, my body warming as we moved together.

Chris moaned into my mouth, and he tasted the way he smelled. A citrus scent and taste making me dizzy as the kiss deepened. Suddenly I realized Chris was walking us backward into my room. The door shut, and he must have kicked it since his arms were wrapped tight around me. A moment later the back of my legs hit the bed, and I fell back on it.

Chris moved closer, so that his body was hovering over mine. He ran his nose along the ridge of my cheek, sending a wave of pleasure through my body. My heart raced as he leaned down to feather kisses across my face and neck.

I tilted my head back and closed my eyes, moaning as Chris's lips kissed me again and again. His groin pressed against mine, and I could feel his hard cock thrusting against me.

The intensity between us heightened as our tongues tangled and explored each other's mouths. A sob escaped me as Chris deepened the kiss and pulled at my bottom lip with his teeth. Suddenly he broke the kiss, and I gasped.

"Don't stop," I breathed, and when I opened my eyes his bright greens were shining down on me. Our breathing had become ragged with desire, but we just looked at each other for a few moments before he captured my lips again in another searing kiss.

My hands moved up to his hair as we continued exploring our mouths, heat radiating off both of us like a furnace. I broke the kiss, and nibbled on his neck. Chris gasped, then he grabbed my arms and we swapped positions. I was on top, and I feathered kisses across his forehead, then kissed each closed eyelid before finding his mouth again.

Our tongues danced in a way I'd never experienced before —almost like they had minds of their own—as we explored each other's mouths with a wild passion I couldn't contain any longer. His hands moved down my back and around to my hips as he pulled me closer to him, deeper into his embrace. Chris broke the kiss once more, leaving me gasping for breath.

"You taste so good…" He whispered against my lips before leaning back in for another mind-blowing kiss that left me nearly paralyzed with pleasure. Chris's cock pushed up into mine, and pleasure spread through my limbs. Then the reality of the situation hit me, and reluctantly, I pushed him away. He slid off me, lying by my side gasping for air.

"Why did you stop?" Chris whispered.

"Trust me, I don't want to." I turned on my side and slid my hand up his shirt until I found a nipple. He groaned when I squeezed it. "I have to be upfront about something first, then we can take this further."

"What?" Chris sighed. My hand slid down his abs, then my fingers slid into his pants, only stopping when they hit the tip of his now-wet cock head.

"I'm very attracted to you, Chris." I moved my hand down further and grasped his girth and squeezed. His hips bucked, and I squeezed harder. "But I moved to Hollywood to focus on my career, and that's my top priority. I need you to understand that. It doesn't mean there isn't a future for us, it just means that I'd prefer to keep things simple for now." I released my grip on his cock, then climbed in between his legs and unzipped his pants.

"I can live with that." Chris whispered, and I unbuttoned the top button of his pants and began to pull them down. "I gotta focus on my career too." He lifted his ass, and I pulled his pants down further. He wore bright-red boxer briefs, and the outline of his thick cock nearly took my breath away. "It's been so long." Chris gasped, and I stood up for a moment. Then I pulled both his underwear and his pants completely off and climbed back in between his legs. I blew a stream of air over his dick, and Chris's hips bucked again. "Oh my God, please, take my cock in your mouth."

Jesus, I'd fantasized about this moment for a very long time. Lonely nights in Boston after I left Virginia were spent imagining him naked in front of me again. I grabbed his length, then licked the head of his cock before taking it in my mouth.

"Yes," Chris hissed. My tongue swirled around it, and with my other hand I pressed the tender skin below his balls. He tasted as good as I remembered, both sweet and salty. I took another inch in my mouth, and was delighted to hear him groan. Slowly I began working his shaft with both my hand and my mouth, and a few moments later Chris gasped and grabbed my head, holding me still.

"Stop, I'm getting close." Chris let go of my head, and when I looked up he began pulling his shirt off. "I want to taste you too, Jett." The shirt fell from his hand to the floor. "Take your clothes off, now."

He didn't have to ask me twice. It took less than ten seconds for me to stand up, rip off my t-shirt, and drop my pants on the floor next to it. Sudden shyness filled me. Something about Chris was different from other guys. I wanted to please him, make him feel better than he ever had before. But I didn't have what he did. No washboard abs, and my skin color was so white compared to his golden tan.

"What's wrong?" Chris lifted his hand. I took it, and he pulled me down on top of him.

"Nothing, I'm just not used to being with…"

"You're gorgeous." Chris feathered his lips across mine. His hands reached into my hair, and he peppered his lips across my jaw. "So fucking beautiful. Don't be shy with me, baby."

Baby. Jesus, he was the only man who'd ever called me that. This was almost like those nights spent in his backseat, making out, then getting each other off with our hands and mouths. The one thing I'd always wanted to do, but we never did, was suck each other off at the same time. That was impossible to do in the back of his beat up VW Beetle, but now we had all the space we needed on my bed.

"You're the gorgeous one, Jett."

I slid down his frame until my mouth was over his swollen cock, then I positioned myself so my cock was next to his face. "I always wanted to try this with you, you know, doing it to each other at the same time." I took the head of his cock in my mouth, then my whole body stiffened when he did the same to me. We both moaned, and the vibration of his mouth on my dick felt so amazing.

Chris's hands, mouth and tongue went to work on my cock, and I nearly forgot to do the same to him. Finally we were sucking each other in unison, the air filled with the sloppy sounds of our mouths working our cocks. Our hips began bucking as the intensity increased, and then I felt that feeling at the base of my groin, and I knew I was about to come. I let his cock slip out of my mouth for a second, and muttered, "I'm almost there."

"Come in my mouth." Jett whispered. Nobody had ever let me do that before, and I decided to do the same to him. Our mouths and hands went back to work, and soon my legs were shaking so much I knew it was only a matter of seconds. I felt Chris's cock stiffen even more, and a little spurt of salty liquid on my tongue told me he was on the verge too. Suddenly, his body went stiff, and a deep groan came from Chris as my mouth filled with his come. My face felt hot, and that heat spread down my body. Jesus, I never knew that another man's come could taste so good. Little sobs escaped me while I swallowed him, then the tingle at the base of my groin became a throb. His cock fell from my mouth, but he never stopped sucking mine.

"Here, here, oh Chris, shit." My eyes snapped shut, and I exploded into his throat. "Oh my fucking God." I groaned through clenched teeth. Chris gripped my hips, holding me in place while he swallowed my come. Then my entire body shook as my orgasm faded away.

"Wow," I breathed, and I could smell the musk coming from Chris's now softening cock. Damn, it was so beautiful, like, it was damn-near perfect. The perfect size, shape, and I could easily become addicted to his scent.

"Come up here," Chris breathed, and for a moment I didn't understand what he wanted. "I want to lay my head on your chest, Jett. In fact, I've wanted to do that since I first saw you at the airport."

Shit. That sounded romantic. If this was any other time or place, I'd be all for it. But my career was my goal. But maybe this once would be alright.

"We don't have to spoon or anything, I just…"

"Shut up." I whispered, then moved my body until it was flat next to him. "I think spooning sounds perfect."

———

I awoke the next morning alone.

"Damn." I hugged the pillow where he'd slept tighter, and I could smell his musky citrus scent all over it. Chris must have left in the middle of the night without a word, and I wished he'd stayed. It would be so easy to fall for him, and if this was another place or time, I would. But until my career took off, that had to be my sole focus.

"Still, this roommate with benefits situation ain't half bad."

I reached down and squeezed my morning wood. If Chris were still here, maybe we could take care of each other's morning boners? Chris tasted so sweet, and that was possibly the most intense orgasm of my life.

"Maybe he's still here, and we could…"

My phone buzzed on the nightstand. I picked it up and saw a message from Marla.

Come to my office ASAP.

CHAPTER 12
CHRIS

I woke up in Jett's arms, and the scent and warmth of his skin made me want to forget about my early morning photo shoot and stay in bed with him. I gently leaned over Jett and noticed his phone on the nightstand. It was 6:30, and if I wanted to make it to the studio on time, I had to get moving.

"I wish I could stay here with you," I whispered with my lips pressed against the back of his neck. The window was slightly open, and a chill morning breeze blew through the bedroom. Reluctantly, I peeled myself off of Jett and got out of bed. After picking up my clothes from the floor, I headed towards the door, but turned back one last time. A sliver of drool stretched from Jett's lower lip to his chin, and the serene look on his face made my heart race.

"Damn it," I muttered, then left his bedroom, gently closing the door behind me. Even his drool was attractive, but we couldn't get serious right now. Jett and I both had too much at stake, and I didn't want to end up like that older woman who drove us home from the airport. Her most successful gig in Hollywood was being a taxi driver.

I hurried to my room and went to the adjoining bathroom to turn on the hot water and let it warm up. After selecting my outfit for the day, I got into the shower and nearly jumped out of my skin. The water was still cold, and I didn't have time to wait for it to warm up.

"Well, this is one way to get rid of morning wood." My teeth chattered, and I grabbed the soap and began washing last night down the drain.

————

The photo shoot ended early, so I decided to head over to the Hollywood Multimedia Acting Academy. Maybe I could sit in on a class while waiting for my first one to begin.

The school was housed in a nondescript concrete building next to an auto parts warehouse. When I pushed open the doors, I was surprised to find the inside completely different from what I'd imagined. The walls were painted in various shades of deep purple and blue, and there were antique couches lined up along one side of the waiting room. A large film projector hung from the ceiling, and posters for student films were plastered on the walls.

I made my way down a corridor illuminated by skylights and entered a sprawling auditorium that looked like it could house at least one hundred students. In the center of the room, there was an instructor's podium with a laptop on it and an array of cameras and lights set up around it.

To my left, there were two dozen students seated in chairs staring intently at their instructor as they talked about camera angles, lighting, sound design, and other aspects of film production. I scanned the lecture hall, searching for the perfect place to settle in. A vacant seat tucked away at the back corner of the room caught my eye, and I quickly claimed it. The instructor was speaking in detail about how utilizing capti-vating visuals could enhance narrative tension within films. I didn't understand most of it, but that was what I was here for, to learn. Since I had time to kill, I decided to stay.

When class let out, I went back to the main waiting area and slowly walked around, eyeing the posters for student films dotting the walls.

"I swear it's him," a woman about my age with thick tortoiseshell glasses whispered to her friend, pointing at me. Since I'd only been a model, I was fairly certain she was mistaking me for someone else. "Look," the woman whipped out her phone and handed it to her friend.

"Oh my God, you're right!" her friend exclaimed and ran over to me. "Is this you?" On her phone was the cover for one of the many romance novels I'd been on.

"Ah, yes," I sighed, feeling a blush race up my neck.

The woman's friend gaped at me. "You're him! I can't believe it!" She grabbed my arm and pulled me along excitedly. "Come on, we have to get a group photo with you."

Four more of the woman's girlfriends squealed and ran over to us.

"We're reading this in our book club," the first woman said, then handed me her phone. "Everyone, get behind him. Would you please take a selfie with us?"

Was this what it was like to be Hugo or Becket? I held the phone up over my head.

"Say cheese!" I grinned, and they all said cheese at once while I snapped the picture.

"And who do we have here?" A middle-aged woman in her fifties strolled up to us.

"Hi Mrs. Adler," the women said at once, then the girl who gave me her phone for the picture snatched it back from me and scampered off with her friends.

The woman wore oversized designer sunglasses and bright orange lipstick that accentuated a tiny mole under her lower lip. She wore head-to-toe black with tiny glittery appliques stitched into the material, with matching ornaments in her brilliant-red hair.

"I'm Priscilla Adler, the director of Hollywood Multimedia Acting Academy." She grinned and held out her hand. I shook it, careful not to squeeze too hard. She had an odd birdlike quality to her. "And you are..."

"Oh, sorry," I grinned. "My name's Chris Reynolds, and today is my first day."

"And why were those girls going mad for you?" She tilted her head.

"I'm a model on the cover of a romance novel they're reading in a book club or something." I blushed, unused to the attention.

"You've got it." Priscilla took my arm in hers and started dragging me out of the reception area. "That rare ability to photograph well. That's half the battle right there. Learning to act is the other battle, and if I'm not mistaken, you're in my next class. Your agent is Marla Fleming, right?"

"Yes, ma'am."

Priscilla stopped in her tracks and glared at me. "Never, ever call me ma'am again. I'm not that old."

"Of course, Mrs. Adler," I attempted to smile at her, but she resumed dragging me down the hall. "So, you're going to teach me how to audition better?"

"Yes."

We arrived at a classroom, and she pushed open the door. Gesturing for me to enter, I did and sat in the back row.

"Nope, that won't do." She was at the front row of chairs and tapped on one of the seats. "Marla told me you need extra attention, so sit up front, please."

Fuck. I hated being singled out, but I didn't have a choice in the matter. I left my seat and strolled to the front.

"As I said earlier, the camera already loves you." She twirled around, and the room began to fill with pupils. "Now we have to make casting directors fall in love with you too."

According to Mrs. Adler, giving a great audition was all about poise, preparation, and perspiration, though the third item shouldn't be noticeable. She also made it plain that I knew none of the above.

Mrs. Adler took off her sunglasses, laid them on the lectern, and scanned the dozen or so students. "Today we have a guest, an actress who is currently under contract with Disney for a retelling of the Cinderella story." She gathered up her belongings from the podium. "It's my pleasure to present you with Tony award-winning actress Goldie Fox!"

A gorgeous woman who appeared to be in her mid-forties walked down the aisle from the back of the class and took her place at the podium. Mrs. Adler sat next to me, patting my arm and smiling.

"Thank you." Goldie smiled, and nothing above her nose moved. I always wondered how actors who'd pumped their faces full of Botox and fillers could actually act. Like, didn't your face need to move to be expressive? "Priscilla and I go way back. She was my understudy on Broadway when I played in Evita." She smiled in our direction, and I wondered if Mrs. Adler was the type of actress who'd deliberately sabotage an actress so she could go onstage in her place. "Unfortunately for her, I didn't miss a performance, but we've been warm friends ever since."

That's when it hit me. Goldie Fox was a friend of Becket and

Hugo's, and I'd been to a couple of small parties at their house where she'd quickly made herself the center of attention.

"I know you," she pointed at me and gave a little wave. The woman was stunning, though like Mrs. Adler, a little over the top. Her long hair was piled on top of her head, held in place by jeweled chopsticks, and she wore an enormous white sweater with Chanel emblazoned on it.

"The key to a fabulous audition is preparation," Goldie said as she slowly walked back and forth across the tiny stage. "You also need to appear confident, even if you don't feel it. Casting directors can smell fear, and it turns them off." Goldie pointed at her chest. "Ask me how I know." The class giggled.

"I'm going to confess something to you. When I first arrived in Hollywood, I couldn't get a job," she said, throwing her hands in the air. "Me, a Tony award-winning actress, couldn't get a job in this town because I lacked confidence."

Hugo had told me it was because she was too old for the parts she auditioned for.

"But Priscilla took this old bird under her wing and taught me how to audition in Hollywood, which is totally different from how you'd do it in New York," she said, gesturing toward Mrs. Adler. "And now I'm under contract at Disney. So let that be a lesson to all of you: Don't be afraid to reach out for help."

"Chris, right?" Goldie asked, and I nodded. After she'd given her little speech, she sat where Mrs. Adler had been before getting back on stage. Class was over, and my brain was over-loaded with everything I'd been taught.

"You look like a deer stuck in bright headlights," she grinned. "Don't worry, you've got what this town wants, and now you have to figure out how to present yourself best. It's hard, but trust me, once you get a foot in the door, the rest will be smooth sailing."

Everyone kept saying that. The cameras loved me. I'd got what it took. But did I really? Because every audition I'd gone to was a dismal failure. Yeah, I might look great on camera, but apparently, I couldn't act my way out of a paper bag.

"Are you going to Becks and Hugo's little going-away party for Candace?" She stood and gestured for me to walk her out of the class. "She's going to be in Guatemala shooting some documentary about migrants. I don't know how she'll survive in the jungle or wherever it is she'll be." She looped her arm through mine, and the few remaining students gawked at us.

"I wasn't invited, but I don't know Candace all that well," I replied. Ever since Becket and Hugo got together, Hugo had been hanging out more with Becket's friends, all successes in Hollywood. Me? I was the dude they let stay in their spare bedroom when the power went out.

"You should crash the party," Goldie laughed, and I held the door open for her. "We need younger faces, though Hugo doesn't look a day over twenty."

"Maybe I will," I smiled, not meaning it. Hugo's new friends intimidated me, though I had to admit it was probably all in my head. While they sipped fancy cocktails and discussed movie contracts and bad plots, I felt like the charity case using them for photos I could post on Instagram.

"I'll talk to Becks and see what I can do." We stepped outside into the bright sunshine, both of us sliding sunglasses on. "You're new in the business, right?"

"Yeah, that's why Marla is making me take these acting classes," I said.

"Marla's excellent," Goldie replied. She pressed a button on her key fob, and the headlights on her BMW flickered on and off. "In fact, I'm thinking about switching to Marla. She's done marvelous things for Hugo, and my agent is practically worthless. It took me years to land this part with Disney, and I'm wondering if she could have sped things up for me a bit." Goldie air-kissed me on both cheeks as she opened her car door. "I'm sure I'll be seeing you soon."

I didn't want Goldie to see me walk out of the parking lot since I hadn't driven. So, I pulled out my phone and acted like I was busy with it until she drove off. Once she was gone, I stuck the phone back in my pocket and strolled to the bus stop. According to the sign next to it, I had almost half an hour before the next bus.

"Shit," I muttered. It was the hottest part of the day, and it was close to ninety degrees outside. I explored the map on the sign and realized it was only a fifteen-minute walk from Flaming Saddles. Would Jett mind if I just showed up where he worked, especially after last night? Or would he think I was coming on too strong? We'd both agreed to keep it light, with no strings attached until we were both more successful.

A dirty guy wearing too many clothes and pushing a grocery cart filled with junk strolled up and sat down on the bench. It broke my heart every time I saw a homeless person in LA, especially since I'd come awfully close to being one. A light breeze blew past us, and the smell coming from the guy was more than I could bear.

"Fuck it," I strolled away in the direction of the bar. "I need a drink."

CHAPTER 13

JETT

"Do you know how much longer Marla's going to be?"

The receptionist smiled. "Any minute now Mr. Sumner. She's anxious to see you, but she has to put out a little fire first." I blanched. "Not your fire, sweetie."

"Thanks," I said, then picked up a magazine from the coffee table in front of me and began thumbing through it. It was an industry journal focusing on public relations. I yawned and put it back.

A buzzer sounded, and Gloria tapped a button on the phone in front of her.

"Send Jett in."

Gloria glanced over to me as I was getting to my feet. "Good luck," she said.

I pushed open the door to Marla's office, and the first thing I noticed was her hair wasn't burgundy anymore. Now it was dark brown, straight, and cut in a very professional bob that stopped right below her jawline.

"Great hair," I muttered, and sat down in the metal and leather chair in front of her desk.

"Thanks," Marla grinned. "I'm glad you're sitting down, because you're going to flip out when I tell you the awesome news I have."

She handed me a stack of papers, and began to explain the details slowly and deliberately, while I tried to comprehend what the documents meant.

"Xist records, a subsidiary of Sony Music International, is offering you a contract. While this is fabulous news, there are a number of things we need to go over first." Marla stood and went to the bar on the other side of her office. "Would you like something to drink? Because this is going to take awhile."

Since it wasn't even noon yet, I decided alcohol was a no-no, even though I wanted to celebrate. "Mineral water, please."

She pulled a bottle out of the fridge and handed it to me before settling behind her desk. "They originally offered a three album deal, but after thinking it through I turned them down."

"What?!"

"Hear me out, Jett." Marla tapped on her computer keyboard for a moment and eyed the screen. "You probably know as much about the music industry as I do, since you've been running your own indie label for a while now. After researching where the industry is headed, I thought perhaps you wouldn't want to be tied to a long-term contract. From what I'm seeing, if we can get a label to properly launch you, we can then make more money by returning to indie."

"I don't get it." I twisted off the top of the water bottle and water fizzled over my hand. "Damn it."

"You're a niche musician, meaning your appeal will primarily be to the LGBTQ community, and to dance-music lovers." She tapped on the keyboard, then turned the computer screen around so I could see it. "What I'm trying to say is unless you completely overhaul your sound to mainstream pop, which I suspect you don't want to do, you'll want to own all the rights to your music and merchandise. A long-term contract with a major label prevents that, since they want to own and control their artists."

"Oh, okay." This made a lot of sense, and obviously Marla had done her homework.

"What I decided on was a three single deal, followed by one album. The singles are released to dance clubs first, followed by the album." She typed on the keyboard, then pointed at the computer screen where she'd highlighted a row of numbers. I stood up and leaned in to see them. "I will email you these numbers along with the contract so you can examine them further. Please, have an attorney look over it before signing the contract. I already had my lawyer study it, but you need an independent set of eyes looking over the numbers too."

"Honestly, this is all very confusing." I sat down and scratched my head.

"I know, it confused me too since this is my first foray into music. So, let me explain this as simply as possible." Marla stood and began pacing around her office. "In my opinion, unless you're a very mainstream artist like Justin Bieber or Taylor Swift, being indie is your best way forward. That way you're in control of everything instead of a number cruncher at Sony."

"Why should I sign this contract if you don't believe it's..."

"Because we can use their money to launch your career." She grinned and rubbed her hands together. "Of course I want you to do your best for Sony for the duration of the contract, but think about it like this. If they can get even one single in the top ten on the dance charts, we can capitalize on that after the contract is over. You're already making a few thousand dollars a month as an indie. Can you imagine how much more you will make after you've got a hit single under your belt?"

"Okay, so you want me to take their money, launch myself to the world at large, and when the contract is up, keep making music but keep all the money for myself."

"Exactly."

"Are they offering an advance?" I asked. "Like, are they prepared to give me money now?"

"Yes, but don't get too excited yet." Marla closed her eyes and took a deep breath. "$250,000."

"Oh my God!" I clutched my chest and started hyperventilating.

"Wait, listen to me before going on a shopping spree." Marla's lips twisted before speaking again. "You receive one third of it when you sign the contract. You get another third when you've completed recording the singles and the album, and the last third when they're released."

This was insane. A bunch of strangers at Sony wanted to just give me a quarter of a million dollars?

"Remember, we want to use their money to launch your career. While I can't tell you how to spend your cash, if you're smart, you won't go spending it on hookers and blow." Marla laughed. "Because, when you go indie, you're the one who has to pay for everything. And to be completely honest, the way this contract is drawn up, you'll never earn a dime of royalties, since you have to pay them back the advance."

"Oh."

"There are a few things you must compromise on, otherwise Sony is withdrawing the offer." Marla said. "And you're probably not going to like what I'm going to say."

I shrugged. For a quarter of a million dollars I'd have sex with Filthy Billy across the hall.

"They insist on you co-writing half of the songs with their

in-house producer, Clint Cash. If you don't know who he is, let me refresh your memory." Marla typed on the keyboard, and a picture of a slightly overweight man in his forties filled the screen. "He's also the producer they want you to work with. If you don't know this already, he's written seventeen top twenty hits, including two number ones by…"

"Mandy Cross." I sighed. "Her music is totally different from mine, like, it's bubblegum pop."

"Yes, but here's the good news. He's got a reputation for working well with artists, and he's not going to take over your sound. But, he'll make your songs as slick and commercial as possible, so Sony makes their money back." She leaned back in her chair and eyed me. "The contract also stipulates you must take dance lessons. Sony watched your live performances on your social media accounts, and insisted you need more polish. I already have an excellent dance instructor in mind. Better yet, the record company is paying for them, so you don't have to."

"Are there any more surprises?"

"No." Marla stared at the ceiling for a moment. "If you do everything Sony wants, I virtually guarantee you'll become a star. And if you don't do something stupid like spend all your money, you'll be set up for a long-term career that will make you a fortune."

———

I stared out at the street from the window of the bus, unable to stop my mind from racing as I considered the offer. It was hard to think straight now that I'd been offered the record deal. All that money, but I was trading my artistic freedom for it. The record company would be in control for at least one album. But for a quarter of a million bucks, I'd do it.

The first thing I wanted to do was go to Flaming Saddles

and quit. I had no intention of telling anyone about the record deal, because I wanted to keep the secret for just a little bit longer, well, except for Chris. Celebrating with him later in bed was what I had in mind.

After getting off the bus in front of Flaming Saddles, I walked up the steps to the bar, opened the door, and strolled inside. Heads turned in my direction, and I felt the familiar wave of anxiousness begin to build in my chest. I hated waiting tables, but today everything felt different. No more assless chaps and hot pink thongs for me, ever again.

"Jett, over here!"

I scanned the bar and saw Chris waving at me from the back. Waving back, I headed in his direction, forcing myself to walk at a slow and steady pace.

"You look like the cat who ate the canary," Chris said, looking me up and down before I sat across from him. "What's up?"

"I just came from Marla's office." I grinned. "Guess who's quitting Flaming Saddles today?"

"What the hell happened?" Chris raised an eyebrow.

"You need to keep this under your hat." I whispered, then saw Gabe staring at us from the bar. He was probably wondering why I wasn't working. "Sony made me an offer." I inhaled deeply. "A quarter of a million dollars, though there are a lot of strings attached."

Chris's mouth dropped open.

"It's for one album and a handful of singles. They want to make me over into a gay Justin Bieber, I think. But for that kind of cash, I'm doing it." I stood up and pointed at Chris's beer. "Finish that now, because in less than five minutes that bear behind the bar is going to be very pissed off at me."

I walked up to the bar and stared into Gabe's eyes.

"Why aren't you in uniform?" He growled.

"I um, quit."

The burly bartender's face turned red. He stepped back from the bar and looked at me in disbelief.

"You mean, you're giving me two weeks notice, right?" He asked, squeezing the wet towel in his hands. "We took a chance on you, and you've made good money here. That's how you want to treat us?"

"I'm quitting right now." My heart raced, because I hate confrontations. Then without thinking, I blurted out, "I was just offered a record deal, and trust me, it's worth way more than what I make here." I spun around, waving at him. "Bye!"

"Get the fuck out, loser!"

––––––

"Well that was a dramatic exit," Chris laughed. "Damn, I'm so happy for you."

We'd walked home from the bar, and our building was only one more block away. The look on Chris's face told a different story than his words.

"Are you okay?" I put my arm over his shoulder, which he promptly shrugged off.

"Yeah, sorry." He shoved his hands in the pockets of his slacks. "It's just, I've been here for years now, and…"

"You want success too." Shit. I'd been so excited to share this with Chris, but I hadn't thought of how he would take it. I reached for him and he pulled back.

"Jett, I'm thrilled for you, trust me. But I feel like I'm never going to be more than a pretty face in a city filled with prettier faces than mine." Chris jogged up the steps of our building and held open the door for me. My head swirled trying to come up with something to make him feel better. I walked past Chris, then turned when we were in front of the elevator.

"It's Marla, I swear she's a genius." I punched the up button. "Listen to her and do everything she says, and I swear it will happen for you too."

We waited for a tense moment, then the doors opened. Chris entered first and I followed, then the elevator doors shut. As always, I felt vaguely nauseous as the car started its trip up.

"So how do you want to celebrate?" Chris winked at me, and my stomach flipped. Perhaps he wasn't as upset as I thought. I knew exactly how I wanted to celebrate, and it involved us getting naked.

Draping my hands over his shoulders, I pulled him in close and kissed the tip of his nose. "Your bed, or mine?"

Chris started to reply but the elevator opened on our floor and we were startled by our neighbor.

"Come back Kitty Purry!"

Filthy Billy was running toward the elevator wearing only a neon yellow bikini. I glanced down and a tiny black kitten with sparkling blue eyes ran in between Chris's feet. He scooped it up and held it in his arms.

"Oh thank God you got her." Billy breathed, and Chris handed him the kitten. Billy held the purring fluff to his cheek and spoke in baby talk.

"No more running away from Daddy!"

CHAPTER 14

CHRIS

The little feline, with its coal-black coat, tufts of fur the color of night, and two sparkling blue eyes, seemed to be begging for attention. As if she needed any more encouragement, the kitten purred softly in a gentle rhythm, and I couldn't help but smile at the sight. In fact it was almost comical, this sleazy older man in a bikini cooing over this precious kitten.

"I named her after my favorite singer, Katy Perry." Billy said, kissing the kitten on her wet nose. "She always has the hunkiest boys in her music videos."

"She's adorable," Jett smiled, and I felt his hand slowly moving along my back.

Billy began rocking the kitten back and forth like an infant, whispering how he would take care of her forever. This was definitely odd behavior for a porn producer. I always imagined them smoking hideous cigars and doing lots of drugs.

"Boys, would you do me a tremendous favor and watch over Kitty Purry for the next couple of weeks while I'm out of town?" Billy smiled at us. "You know, just pick up my mail, make sure Kitty is fed and watered. Oh, and play with her. I don't want her to be lonely while I'm gone."

"Eew. Litter boxes." I mumbled, and Jett kicked my ankle. "Ouch!"

"No problem Billy," Jett reached a hand out and stroked Kitty's tiny head. "At this age, the litter box is no problem." Jett winked at me. "Tiny kittens have tiny poop."

"Oh, yeah." I shrugged. My mother never allowed us to have pets, so I didn't know much about the care and feeding of tiny panthers. "Where are you going, Billy?"

"Filming my next cinematic masterpiece, The Boys of Anchorage."

I snickered, and Billy winked at us.

"From the online applications I've received so far, men in Alaska are steamy hot." Billy's eyes took on a wondrous gleam. "They all look like lumberjacks, well, the pictures with their clothes on, that is."

Jett leaned over and pecked Kitty Purry on her head. "We look forward to babysitting for you."

"Bye, Kitty," I waved at the black fluff, then we walked to our door and Jett let us in. Once the door closed, Jett licked his lips and seconds later I was pinned against the wall. His warm breath tickled my neck as he murmured into my ear. "We should celebrate," he breathed. Then he brushed his lips across mine, soft and gentle, sending a tingle of pleasure through my body.

Jett's hands suddenly moved from my waist to behind my head and tilted it so our mouths met in a passionate kiss. His tongue explored every inch of my mouth, sending shivers down my spine. Jett's hands moved down to my thighs, and my cock immediately firmed up. I grabbed him by the elbow and dragged him down the hall, passing his bedroom. When we got to my room I let him go, fell back on the bed and grinned.

"It's time to party, baby."

————

This was perfect. I gently kissed the back of Jett's head, wishing I didn't have to get ready for work. We'd spent the night making love, then talking for hours about our ambitions. The smell of his hair, something in between a field of flowers and citrus fruits, was intoxicating. My morning wood pressed against his back, and I wanted nothing more than to call Marla and lie to her. Tell her we'd both contracted a bug or a virus, anything to stay here together.

But, that wasn't meant to be. We were determined to make it in Hollywood, and the only thing holding us back was ourselves.

Jett mumbled something in his sleep, then turned on his back. I scooted back, stared at his perfect, angular face, and for the first time wondered what it would be like if neither of us wanted to be a star.

We could move back home to Richmond and start all over again. I could ask Dad for a job where he worked, or just get any old job. Waiting tables was out of the question, but I could work in retail. Jett already knew how to run a small independent business. Maybe he could open up a cafe, or be content playing small gigs around the state. The pressure would be gone. No more agents, acting classes, and feeling worthless every time I fucked up an audition.

Living in Hollywood was so damned hard. Everyone was out for something, and if you couldn't help them, they wanted nothing to do with you. It didn't matter how nice you were, all that mattered was how you looked. Yes, talent was important, but as I was coming to realize, it didn't matter much in the scheme of things. Trust me, there were tons of actors in this town who scratched out a living, not because of talent, but because they gave casting directors a boner.

"Am I doing this for all the wrong reasons?" I whispered, and Jett shifted next to me. Honestly, I never imagined myself being a great actor. But I didn't have anything other than my looks to fall back on. That made me feel so fucking shallow.

When I was a kid, nobody encouraged me to excel at academics. Why? Because I was attractive, and came from an upper-middle-class family with connections. I wasn't expected to be great at anything, because people like me skated through life without having to work hard.

Honestly, I could tell Marla to just keep booking me decent modeling gigs and I'd still make a good living without acting. But now that Jett was in my life, with his ambitions to be a pop star, I felt like I had to do more. To be better than I was. Did I really want to go through life coasting, or did I have what it took to actually be a good actor?

Slowly, so I wouldn't wake him, I climbed out of bed and tiptoed to the bathroom door. I opened it, then turned back, staring at Jett's innocent face.

Would Jett still want me if I wasn't a star? I mean, we weren't serious, but if we were, would I be enough for him just being myself?

———

"My skin smells like fucking coconuts," I bitched while opening the door to our building. I went to acting class in the morning, where I learned how to fake understanding a script on command. Then I went to a photoshoot for the International Male catalog. It specialized in sexy underwear, and I'd spent the afternoon being sprayed with oil to make my skin glow.

The photoshoot had been okay, but the oil was cloying and I wanted a hot shower more than anything else in the world. I groaned as I swung open the door to our building, two heavy shopping bags dangling from my fingers. Jett texted me to pick up some groceries from the store before coming home, so that's what I'd done. Nothing healthy, just a couple of frozen pizzas and a six pack of beer. He said he would've done it himself but a song he was working on was driving him crazy, and he couldn't make himself stop.

When the elevator doors opened on my floor, I was greeted by Kitty Purry.

"Hi, beautiful," I put down one of the bags and rubbed her cheek. Billy's door was open, and I heard 70s disco music coming from his apartment.

"Kitty is very social," Billy's head popped out of his doorway. "She likes wandering the hallway and saying hello to the neighbors."

"As long as the neighbors don't mind, I don't." I picked up the bag and went to my door. Thank God Billy had normal clothes on for a change. Well, for him. Billy wore a bright Hawaiian shirt open to his belly button, and for the first time I realized his nipples were pierced. He had on a pair of khaki clam diggers that came down to his mid-calf, and a pair of green espadrilles.

Kitty ran in between my feet as soon as I got the door open. I dropped the bags and picked her up. "No, little Kitty. Time to go home."

I handed her to Billy with a smile. "Talk to you later. Jett and I are heading out soon."

I shut the door before the conversation could drag on further, and heard Jett's guitar in the background, and what sounded like a string orchestra. "Can't imagine him fitting one of those in his room."

I dropped off the groceries in the kitchen, then went to his bedroom door. Instead of knocking, I pressed my ear against the door. That was when I heard his voice begin to sing over the music.

Every time I look at you, my heart begins to race
  I'm drawn to you like the sun to an open space
  I've tried to fight these feelings, but they just won't go away
  I'm falling deeper every day, what more can I say?
  I'm in love with you, there's no denying
  My heart beats faster when you're near
  I've been trying to hide it, but now I'm trying
  To tell you how I feel
  I never thought I'd feel this way about another man
  But every time I'm with you, I know that I can
  Be myself and be accepted, for who I truly am
  I never knew love could be so simple and so grand

A soft drum roll accompanied by a piano played, then Jett resumed singing.

I'm in love with you, there's no denying
  My heart beats faster when you're near
  I've been trying to hide it, but now I'm trying
  To tell you how I feel
  I know this might be hard to hear
  But I had to let you know
  I don't want to live in fear

Of what could be, or letting go
I'm in love with you, there's no denying
My heart beats faster when you're near
I've been trying to hide it, but now I'm trying
To tell you how I feel
I hope you can see what I see
And maybe feel what I feel too
If not, that's okay with me
I'll still be here, loving you.

The strings faded, and I heard Jett moving around. That's when I felt a tear sliding down the side of my nose, and I brushed it off.

"Shit," I whispered. I didn't want him to think I was spying on him, so I tiptoed back to the kitchen. God, his voice was so beautiful, but more than that were the lyrics. I knew he could be writing them about anyone, or no one at all.

"Hey, you're home!" Jett grinned from the kitchen doorway. "Today was amazing. I think I wrote a song my new producer is going to love." He strolled up to me and sniffed. "What's that smell?"

I sighed. "Coconut oil. I modeled underwear today and they kept spraying me down with oil so my skin would be shiny in the pics." Damn it, now I couldn't get those lyrics out of my head. "Hey, I've um, gotta meet someone. There's beer in the fridge, and some frozen pizza. I'll be back in a little while."

"Is everything okay?" Jett tilted his head, and all I wanted to do was kiss his full lips. But after hearing that song, maybe I needed some distance. This was supposed to be a fling, and suddenly it felt like that wasn't enough.

"Yeah," I moved past him, and our chests touched for a moment. Sweat dripped down my sides. "I'll be back soon.

Can't wait to listen to your new song." I called over my shoulder, then hurried out of the apartment.

Kitty Purry was still in the hallway, playing with a stuffed toy too big for her. When I got on the elevator I turned and saw Jett's face from our doorway, staring at me. Then the elevator doors shut, and pressure built under my eyes.

"What if that song was about me?"

CHAPTER 15

JETT

Waking up alone sucked.

My eyes fluttered open and I yawned, not feeling rested at all. I picked up the cell phone from my nightstand and reread the short text message Chris had sent me last night.

> Spending the night with Hugo and Becks.
> Don't wait up.

There was no explanation, because we were only friends. No commitment, no strings, just two friends who had extremely hot sex. That was what I wanted, right? In fact, I was the one who insisted on it.

Both of us were at the beginnings of our careers, and we, no, I must focus solely on making myself a star. Could we get involved? Yes, but now was a bad time.

"I miss him."

The bed felt empty without Chris, and the knot in my stomach grew bigger with every passing second. I rolled over and felt a pang of sadness in my chest, and wondered why Chris had left the way he did yesterday.

Was it the song? I hadn't played it for him, but what if he'd heard me singing it in my bedroom? Even if he had heard it, how could he guess it was about him?

"Damn it," I turned over and punched the pillow. The song was about Chris, and I couldn't deny it. Songwriting was similar to acting. Like acting, you took emotions you were feeling or had felt before, and you used those feelings to craft songs. And I had to admit, being with Chris the last few weeks had triggered emotions I'd never felt before. Even when we were teenagers, we'd always put our professional ambitions first. That was why I'd moved to Boston for school, and it was why Chris had moved to Hollywood.

But even though I suspected Chris was reacting to the song, I couldn't be sure. For all I knew Chris went to Hugo and Becks's house to have a hot threesome, or he drank too much while he was hanging out with his celebrity friends and decided to crash in their guest room.

"We're not in a relationship, so unless he chooses to tell me where he was and why, it's none of my business."

I got out of bed and opened the window, breathing in the cool morning air. The skin on my arms pebbled when a breeze came through, and I sat on the edge of the bed and drew the blankets around me.

"What if he feels the same?" I whispered, then my phone pinged. It was my calendar, reminding me of how very busy my life was becoming. Today I meet with my new producer/songwriter Clint Cash. Then I had dancing class with some lady named Tonia Bianchi. What the hell do you even wear for dance lessons?

This was why I couldn't get involved with Chris or anyone

else right now. I had too much to do, and too much at stake to allow myself the luxury of falling in love.

I stood up, letting the blanket slide off me and onto the floor.

"My commitment is to my career, and once that's settled, then I can fall in love." I walked to the bathroom, opened the door, and stared at my exhausted reflection in the mirror. "Damn it, why does it always feel like the wrong time with me and Chris?"

———

My Uber driver dropped me off at the entrance of an immense gated property and my jaw nearly hit the sidewalk. "Jesus Christ, is this a mansion or a recording studio?" The driver shook his head and drove away.

I stood there for a few moments, taking in the grandeur of it all. The house was surrounded by lush gardens and tall trees that provided shade from the blazing California sun. I pushed the buzzer next to the gate.

"How may I help you?" A man's voice with a British accent came out of the speaker.

"It's Jett Sumner. I have an appointment with..." The gate opened, and I followed a stone path towards the front door, still feeling overwhelmed at what stared back at me.

When I knocked on the huge wooden door, I heard the sound echoing through it. A few seconds later, a tall man with bright blue eyes and gray hair pulled back in a ponytail, opened it. He smiled at me warmly, and said, "You must be Jett."

"Hi," I held my hand out.

The man took a lit joint from his fingers, put it between his lips, and shook my hand. "Nice to meet you. I'm Clint."

"Before we hit the studio, let's talk for a little bit." Clint led me through a maze of hallways. We passed several rooms with gleaming instruments and top-of-the-line equipment before finally reaching his office.

It was spacious, with high ceilings and large bay windows along one of the walls. Two retro lamps glowed against the light from outside, casting beams of warm light across the room. The walls were lined with vintage vinyl records and books, and the ashtray on his enormous wood desk was overflowing with stubbed out joints.

"Please, have a seat." Clint gestured toward the leather chair in front of the desk.

My pulse raced, because I was sitting in front of a man responsible for so many hit songs. Now he's going to both judge the songs I've written, and hopefully make one of them a hit.

"Want to smoke?" Clint opened a wooden cigar box, but instead of cigars it was filled with perfectly rolled joints.

"No thanks, um, I can't work under the influence. It throws me off somehow." I replied, not telling him the truth, that I'd never gotten high before.

"Admirable," Clint shut the box, sat back in his chair and grinned. "Wish I could say the same. So, Jett, what are you looking for me to do for you? Obviously we need to record a hit song."

Last night I'd gone over this scenario repeatedly in my head, when I wasn't missing Chris.

"Yeah, a hit song would be excellent," I smiled. "But I want more than that. You're one of the best producers in the business, and a legendary songwriter. I want to learn what makes a hit song so I can write as many as possible."

Clint took a long drag off his joint, then stubbed it out. "I'm not immune to flattery, so that's an excellent answer." He chuckled, then crossed his arms over his chest, letting them rest on his slight beer gut. "I spent last night listening to your work, and going over your social media. You're one of the rare artists who doesn't need much polishing. The songs you've written so far are great pop, so what I'm going to do is make them more danceable. The gays love the clubs, and I want to transform you into the next Erasure, or Pet Shop Boys. Do you know who they are?"

I snickered. "Yes, oh my God. Who doesn't know who they are?" Wow. This man knew exactly what I wanted to sound like, and both of those bands had careers spanning decades.

"Some of you young guys don't know about the older acts. I swear the young queers only listen to Beyoncé and Rhiannon. We're going to change that." Clint typed something into his desktop computer, and a familiar melody filled the air from hidden speakers. It took me a moment, then my jaw dropped open.

"Is that me?" I whispered.

My voice had been digitally altered somehow. It was smoother, sparklier, with just the right amount of effects to make it sound like I was singing in a club instead of my bedroom.

"Yup, that's you." Clint beamed with pride as he adjusted the volume on the speakers. "Got rid of some of your vocal flaws and added just the right amount of effects to make it truly shine."

I couldn't believe what I was hearing--this was my song, but it sounded so much better. "I'm impressed," I smiled at him. "You really know what you're doing."

Clint smirked. "That's why people like me get paid so much." He chuckled, then waved his hand in my direction as if to say 'go on.' "Tell me what else you want out of our collaboration."

I thought for a moment before responding. What did I really want out of this? Sure, having a hit single would be great, but I wanted something even more than that--a chance to learn from one of music's greatest minds. "I want us to work together to create something special," I said finally, trying not to sound too eager or naive. "Something that won't just be heard for one summer, but will live on for years."

Clint grinned and nodded his head in agreement. "That's exactly what I'm looking for too," he said enthusiastically and clapped his hands together. "That's why I mentioned Pet Shop Boys. The reason for their longevity is the quality of their work, and you're the first artist I've met in years who reminds me of them."

There was a knock at the office door. When I turned toward it a skinny woman in her forties with long graying hair stood in the doorway.

"Clint, do you want lunch served in here, or in the studio?" The woman grinned at me.

"Jett, this is my wife, Serena." Clint stood, and gestured for me to do the same. "Send lunch to the studio. Me and Jett have a lot of work to do."

I could've played in Clint's studio all day, but unfortunately for me I had dance class. And as much as it pained me to admit it, when Clint played one of my homemade videos, I realized just how awkward I was on stage.

"Even if you never learn how to really dance, your instructor will at least teach you how to move more naturally." He said as I was leaving, and when I got to the front door he placed a couple of joints in my shirt pocket. "You deserve them, kiddo."

———

Inside the Uber, I got a text from Marla.

> Check your bank balance. DO NOT GO ON A
> SHOPPING SPREE!

I forced myself not to look. Spending the advance could fuck things up for my future.

"We're here." The Uber driver announced as we pulled up to a wooden house a block away from Paramount Studios. When I got out of the car I smelled burnt air from a distant forest fire. There were small potted plants on the porch, and the door was a bright scarlet color. Over it was a sign that said Pineapple Dance Studio.

"Here goes nothing," I muttered, then knocked on the door. I heard feet moving across a wood floor, then the door opened. A tall, thin Italian woman in yellow leotard and tights grinned at me. "Are you Jett?"

"Yes," I mustered up a smile. "Are you Tonia Bianchi?"

"Come in," She stood back and gestured for me to move forward. I stepped inside, and heard bizarre music coming from the next room. It had a definite beat, lush strings, and if my ears heard right, sitars.

"What is that music?" I asked.

"Oh, you're in for a treat," Tonia grinned. "One of my favorite actors is rehearsing for an upcoming Bollywood film." She slowly circled me, then tapped my chest. "You aren't wearing appropriate attire for dance class. So what I'm going to do is let you sit in on this rehearsal so you get a feeling for it, and I'll provide you with a list of things you need for your first official rehearsal."

"I'm so sorry I didn't know what to..."

"Don't worry, honey, your record label is paying for the

lessons, whether you dance or not." She winked, then took my elbow and led me to a door on the other side of the room. When she opened it, I was greeted by the sight of an extremely handsome Indian man and an older woman I kind of recognized dancing to the strange and wonderful music. "They're rehearsing a type of dance known as Bhangra." She whispered. "It originated in Punjab, India and it's a very athletic type of dance. It's typically performed during weddings and other celebrations. Ram's doing it in his next film, and his friend, Goldie, just likes to dance." She giggled.

The man was amazingly graceful and powerful. His movements were sharp, but fluid. The woman was equally impressive. She moved with the same precision and speed, getting into all the nooks and crannies of the choreography without missing a beat.

"Oh, I recognize her from..."

"Broadway," Tonia cut me off. "She's getting ready to shoot a musical for Disney."

I watched in awe as they danced together, each movement seemingly more beautiful than the last until finally they finished with a triumphant flourish that left me breathless.

Tonia clapped her hands together in appreciation before turning to me with a warm smile. "Now that is what Bhangra looks like when it's done properly!"

Ram Khapoor, that was who he was. He was a celebrity friend of Hugo's, and I'd seen pictures of him on social media along with the woman.

"Your next dance class is tomorrow afternoon. Athletic wear is fine, but make sure the clothes aren't loose fitting. It can get in the way of movement." Tonia ordered, and Ram and the woman plucked towels off the bench by the wall, mopping sweat from the back of their necks.

"You two are amazing dancers," I smiled at them. "Aren't you guys friends with Hugo Zepeda?"

"Ah, yes." The woman smiled and shook my hand. "You must be Jett. Chris told us last night you were starting dance lessons. I'm Goldie."

I wonder what else Chris told them about me.

"Ram." The man had a brilliant smile, and when I shook his hand I was a little starstruck. "What a coincidence you're learning from our teacher Tonia. She's the best."

My phone pinged, and when I pulled it out of my pocket, I saw a message from Chris. When I read it, I nearly dropped it to the floor.

We need to talk

CHAPTER 16

CHRIS

After leaving the apartment, I wandered the streets for a while, trying to get my feelings in check. It was surprisingly quiet, and I ended up in an alley off Olvera Street. Street lights cast a dim glow over the deserted alleyway, the only sounds I heard were my heavy footsteps and the occasional car horn.

"What the hell just happened?" I whispered.

The song, the words, the tears I'd bottled up inside. It was too much. I felt so confused. I wished I could just run away and forget it ever happened, but I was stuck in that moment, living it in my head over and over.

The street lights flickered, and I looked up at the night sky, the stars barely visible through the city lights. It was supposed to be a beautiful night. But here I was, feeling like the world was crumbling at my feet.

"I have to go back," I sighed. Jett and I needed to talk this over, because our simple friends with benefits situation was transforming into so much more than that.

"Not yet."

THE BIG TIME   111

Not tonight. I need to process this shit, because none of it was making sense. I'd never had a proper boyfriend before, unless you counted the summer after Jett and I graduated. But that summer didn't feel nearly as intense as what I was feeling now.

A couple of guys entered the alley, dressed in black. My guard immediately went up, so I picked up my pace, walking past them back onto Olvera Street next to the Mexican market. Across the street was a park, and since there was still a little light left in the sky I walked through the entrance framed by two large oak trees. I sat down on a bench, the cold metal seeping through my slacks. Leaning back, I shut my eyes and tried to get my breathing under control.

"I can't lose my friendship with Jett." I rubbed my eyes, then felt my phone ping. It was a text message from Hugo.

> Come to my place. Impromptu party. Bring Jett.

"Yeah, bring Jett," I muttered. I wouldn't do that, but maybe this was exactly what I needed, just a night out with Hugo, Becks, and their weird celebrity friends. Hell, Marla would approve, and tell me to take tons of pics for social media.

I tapped out a message telling Hugo I was on my way, then wondered if I should let Jett know I wouldn't be coming home. Hell, if I could I'd spend the night in one of Hugo's guest rooms. I typed a message and sent it to Jett.

> Spending the night with Hugo and Becks. Don't wait up.

_____

"Chris, it's great seeing you again." Becks hugged me, then stepped back, grabbed my shoulders, and tilted his head. "This is a party, not a wake. What's wrong?"

I'd swear I'd never get used to being hugged by movie stars, much less having one actually concerned with my wellbeing.

"Um, well..."

"Hey, dude, what do you want to drink?" Hugo dragged me away from Becks, then whispered, "Where's Jett? Marla wanted him here too for social media bullshit."

"He's at the apartment." I felt my shoulders droop. "Beer and a shot of tequila would really hit the spot right now."

"Did you two have a fight or something?" Hugo put his arm over my shoulder and walked us outside. Next to the infinity pool a bar had been set up, manned by an actual bartender. Must be nice.

"No, it wasn't a fight." I shrugged his arm off and turned to the bartender. "I'll have a beer and a shot of Cuervo."

The bartender nodded, then grabbed the bottle of tequila and poured me a shot. Hugo watched me as I tossed it back, then the bartender handed me the beer with a look of concern on his face.

"Spill it, dude, what did you two do? Or more importantly, not do?" Hugo raised an eyebrow at me expectantly as he took a sip from his own beer bottle.

I took a deep breath and stared at the lights reflecting off the rippling water before us. "It's complicated."

"I thought you two were just friends?"

"We, you know, kind of started sleeping together again." I sat on a bench next to the pool, and Hugo sat next to me.

"Again?"

"We dated the summer after we graduated high school. But we never allowed it to become serious because he was moving to Boston to go to music school. I knew I'd eventually end up here in LA, so it made sense at the time." I drained half the beer bottle at once, and belched. "Excuse me."

"Well, obviously you two have some chemistry. What's keeping you apart now?" Hugo asked, then waved toward Ram and that crazy actress, Goldie.

"He wants to keep things light until his career takes off. I agreed to it because..."

Goldie strolled up wearing impossibly high heels and a shimmering gown totally unsuitable for a pool party. She smiled widely at us both before giving me an especially knowing look. "Well, hello, boys," she said with a mischievous grin.

"Hey, Goldie," Hugo greeted her with a polite nod of his head.

I just stared at her, not sure what to say or do in such close proximity to acting royalty. Even though we'd met before, I'd never get used to being around stars.

Goldie laughed at my expression before continuing on her way towards the bar.

Hugo patted me on the back sympathetically. "So, if you really like Jett, why not take a chance? Life's too short to just wait around for things to happen."

"Because he made it clear he doesn't want more than a fuck buddy, and for the first time, I don't think that's enough for me." Draining the rest of my beer, I stood up. "I need more of this." I held up my beer bottle and headed toward the bar. When I got there, someone tapped on my shoulder. I ignored it, then Marla's voice jolted me out of my thoughts and back into reality. "Well, hello there," she said with a sly smile on her face as she air-kissed both my cheeks in greeting. She looked so different now that she was a successful Hollywood agent— more polished and powerful.

Marla raised an eyebrow, crossed her arms across her chest

and leaned against the bar next to me. "Where's Jett?" She signaled the bartender, who brought her a bottle of water. "The exposure of being seen at this party will do both of you a lot of good on social media."

I opened my mouth and nothing came out.

"Are you fucking him?" Marla nodded slowly before narrowing her eyes at me. "Look," she said softly but firmly, "you know what they say—you don't get what you don't ask for. If you want him, go for it. And personally, I believe a relationship between the two of you would be excellent publicity."

"What do you mean?" I stammered. Swear to God this woman never thought about anything but publicity.

"Jett is openly gay, and a musician on the rise. You are a model and an actor, also on the rise. After Hugo and Becks's success as an out-and-proud couple, I've seen how wonderful the hype is surrounding their relationship. I want the same thing for you and Jett."

I sighed and stared down at my beer bottle thoughtfully as Marla's words sank in slowly but surely. If I wanted something more with Jett—something real and lasting—I needed to tell him the truth. I began peeling the label off the bottle, and Marla swatted my hand.

"It's so fucking complicated," I grimaced, then got the bartender's attention and pointed at my empty beer bottle. He pulled one out of a sinkful of ice and handed it to me.

"Well, let's leave your personal life out of this for a moment, because I have good news." Marla took a sip of water and grinned. "I got you a commercial!"

I knew I should be thrilled, but I could only muster up a weak smile.

"It's nothing much, but it's a start. You're going to be promoting some idiotic video game, can't remember which one. It's only a fifteen second spot, but the job will hopefully open more doors." She took my elbow and steered us to an empty bench.

"I've also got some ideas for other projects you could be involved in," Marla continued, tapping her fingers on her water bottle. "I want you to audition for a part in Hugo's next movie, and I'm insisting that you audition with Hugo." She waved at someone, then focused on me again. "You two are great friends, and I'm hoping that will make it easier for you in front of the camera. It's a supporting role, so there's not as much pressure."

"Wow, are you serious?" I couldn't believe what she was saying—an opportunity like this rarely happened for me.

Marla nodded vigorously before finishing off her water. "Of course," she said confidently. "But that's only if you're willing to put in the work. You'll have to practice your lines over and over until you have them down pat."

"Yeah, I'll do whatever it takes to get the part." My heart pounded, and for the first time since that unfortunate encounter with Jett, I felt hope.

"Most importantly, though," she said, "you need to show up at auditions looking confident yet approachable—and always be open to criticism and suggestions from directors or fellow actors."

I gulped nervously, but nodded my head in agreement nonetheless; Marla was right—if I wanted this part, then I needed to give it my all. And it was the perfect excuse not to think of Jett.

Ram strolled up to the pool with Goldie on his arm. He had a fork in his hand, and began banging it against his cocktail glass.

"Attention!" He yelled, then pointed at Marla. "No more industry talk tonight! It's time to party!"

———

The rest of the night was a blur. After enduring what seemed like a thousand pictures snapped by Marla for Instagram, I vaguely recalled Hugo dragging me off to one of his guest rooms and putting me to bed. Apparently I'd drunk one too many shots of tequila, and was in the middle of taking my clothes off to go for a swim when he stumbled over and saved me from making a very public fool of myself. According to my phone it was nearly four in the afternoon, and I'd slept my hangover off. Two bottles of water were on the nightstand, along with a couple of aspirin. I ignored the aspirin, and opened a bottle of water.

"I need to speak with Jett." Staring up at the ceiling, I realized I couldn't keep things light and simple mwith him. If all he wanted was a friend with benefits, he'd better find someone else. I grabbed my phone and typed out a simple message, crossed myself, and hit send.

We need to talk

CHAPTER 17

JETT

Ever since I got the text message from Chris, a cloud of worry surrounded me. I knew he was safe with Hugo and Becks, but without any subtext, the message sounded ominous. I clicked on the message and read it again.

> We need to talk.

"What the hell do we need to talk about?" I shook my head, put my headphones on, and began polishing a demo I wanted to play for Clint tomorrow. This was what I needed to worry about, not Chris, or any other guy for that matter. Yes, I found Chris incredibly handsome, and the attraction was definitely mutual. But for the first time in my life I had a famous record producer working on my songs. If I didn't focus on my career right now, I might never have this chance again.

The beat was moving, the melody catchy, and all in all it was good, but it needed something to make it jump out of dance floor speakers. I turned up the bass drum, then the snare. No change. I added hand claps, a cowbell and some backing vocals, and suddenly the song felt ready for prime time. Well, at least it sounded good enough to present to Clint.

Now I needed to go over the lyrics and make sure they stood up under my producer's scrutiny. My voice sounded a little overwhelmed now that I'd pumped up the rhythm section, so I raised the volume on the vocal track.

I had the love of my life
But I let it slip away
Now I'm standing here alone
Wondering what to do or say
You passed me by, oh love of mine
I didn't know what I had
Now I'm dancing in the dark
Hoping that you'll come back

"I'm not sure about the dancing in the dark line," I muttered, and continued listening.

I can't forget the way we moved
Our bodies in perfect sync
But now I'm dancing all alone
And it just makes me think
I can't stop thinking about you
And what we used to be
I'll keep dancing until you're here
To share this dance with me

You passed me by, oh love of mine
I didn't know what I had
Now I'm dancing in the dark
Hoping that you'll come back

I'll keep dancing until the end

Hoping for another chance
To be with the love of my life
And finally find true romance.

I sighed and slumped back in my chair. This was supposed to be an upbeat, feel-good dance track – why did it keep reminding me of Chris?

I ran my fingers through my hair, trying to focus on the task at hand. I wanted to get this song finished before meeting Clint at the studio tomorrow. I looked over what I had so far, and it wasn't bad. The melody was catchy enough, and the rhythm section was bumping—but something was missing, and I just couldn't figure out what it was.

Suddenly it hit me—this song needed a bridge to break up the monotony of verse-chorus-verse and give it some extra oomph. But what kind of bridge should I use? Should I go with a rap verse or something more melodic? Would it even work?

I quickly punched in some chords on my keyboard and started humming along until suddenly the right notes popped into my head. Now all that was left was to write some lyrics that would fit perfectly with the music. I grabbed my pen and notebook, and after a moment the words flowed.

You never know what you got 'til it's gone
But if you're lucky you'll find someone who loves you
So don't wait around for your love
Let go and give yourself a chance
Don't let history repeat itself
Cause life moves too fast for you not to dance

I sat back and savored the moment, feeling proud of what I'd just created. I couldn't believe how easy it had been - everything seemed to flow naturally, like a puzzle piece that finally found its place. All I needed to do was record it and stick the bridge in between the verse and chorus.

"Now if my life could be this simple, everything would be perfect." I sighed. Chris wanted more than I was prepared to give, and I couldn't handle the pressure right now. The lyrics reflected it, kind of. "You never know what you've got 'til it's gone." I knew what I had, I thought. A friend who graciously let me move into his apartment, who stirred feelings in me I'd never felt before. But I had too much going on for anything serious.

"For Christ's sake, Marla's already booking club dates all over California. I don't have time for a boyfriend." I picked up my notebook and tossed it across the room. What do I say to Chris if a relationship is what he wants?

The knot in my stomach vibrated. I checked my bank balance last night, and I could easily afford my own place now. Did I want to go? No. But if I was torturing Chris with my presence, I'd leave.

"Trust me, Chris." I got up and retrieved my notebook. "Hurting you is the last thing I want to do."

———

I was reheating a sandwich when I heard the key turning in the lock. My stomach clenched, and I prayed Chris didn't want to talk right now. Or if he did, all he wanted was to shoot the shit. It would be even better if all Chris wanted was to take my hand and drag me to his bedroom.

A moment later Chris's frame filled the doorway.

"Hey," He mumbled, his eyes on the floor.

"Um, did you have fun with Hugo and all the A-listers?"

"Yeah, kind of." Chris glanced up, then strolled past me and grabbed a bottle of water out of the fridge. "They're really over the top compared to people back in Richmond." He twisted the top off the bottle and sipped. Chris locked eyes with me, inhaled, then said, "We really do need to talk."

Damn it, I really didn't want to have this conversation now.

"Hey, you gotta hear this new song I'm working on, it's..."

"No." Chris leaned against the counter next to me. The microwave dinged, startling both of us. "Jesus, that scared me. Look, this thing we have going on between us. Is it just me, or does it feel like more than sex?"

God, he was so gorgeous. Like, if this was another time or place I'd be thrilled to explore a relationship with him. For fuck's sake, he was a model, totally sex on a stick. But now wasn't the right time, and if I wasn't honest with him, he might never forgive me.

"No," I said finally. "It's not just sex. At least, not on my end."

Chris's expression softened and he closed the gap between us and put his hands on my hips. He leaned in and brushed his lips over mine, then Chris pulled away and smiled. "But?"

I smiled weakly and took a deep breath. It was time to be honest. We both needed that from one another if we were going to keep living together as friends instead of becoming enemies or worse: awkward roommates who never talked to each other again because of unresolved feelings.

"Chris," I began tentatively. "The truth is: I'm a mess right now with my career taking off. Marla's already scheduling dates for a club tour, and I'm just starting to record the songs with my producer. My head isn't really in the right space for a relationship now."

Chris nodded slowly, his eyes locked on mine as he processed what I said. He let go of me and stepped away. "I get that," he said softly. "Touring and recording will take up a lot of your time. But, well, I can't keep sleeping with you if that's all you want from me." Chris glanced away, and I noticed his eyes were wet. "I'm not mad at you or anything, but I need more than sex."

My heart sank as Chris walked away. I was torn between wanting to keep things the way they were—comfortably casual —and not wanting to lose him as a friend. I stepped forward and grabbed his hand, stopping him before he could leave.

"Chris." I said softly. He looked back at me, his eyes still shimmering with emotion. "I'm sorry," I continued, squeezing his hand gently. "Everything's happening so fast, and it's hard for me to think beyond what's right in front of me," I explained. "My career must be my primary focus."

His shoulders slumped, and guilt tore through my guts. How could I hurt him, when all he'd ever done was be my friend? Chris let go of my hand and began walking down the hallway toward his room.

"If you want me to, I'll move out." I babbled, immediately knowing it was the wrong thing to say. "This is really uncomfortable, and I don't want to hurt you, Chris. But I can't give you more than what we have already. I'm so sorry, but..."

He stopped in front of his bedroom door, and without turning to face me, he said, "No, it's okay." His voice dropped. "I just wish things could be different, that's all." He turned the doorknob, walked inside, and shut it.

"Fucking feelings," I muttered, and a tear slid down my cheek. Swiping it away, I trudged back to the kitchen, grabbed my food out of the microwave, and headed back to my room.

———

It was difficult switching off my emotions, meaning it was fucking hard to get any work done. I also felt awkward singing any meaningful lyrics knowing Chris was across the hall. I'd hurt him, the man who'd taken me in after not seeing or talking to him in years. This was how I repaid him? By rejecting him?

"I gotta get out of here."

Grabbing my leather jacket, I quietly opened my bedroom door and shut it, hoping Chris didn't hear me. When I got to the front door, someone knocked.

"Shit," my hand flew to my chest. Chris opened his door and peered down the hall at me. I shrugged. Chris strolled down the hall, gingerly stepped around me, and opened the door.

"Hello, boys," Billy grinned, then his smile flatlined. "Did I come at a bad time?"

"Uh, no, we were..."

"Kitty Purry, come back here!" Billy cried as the kitten raced into our apartment. "Oh dear." He pushed past me and began chasing the bundle of fluff through our living room. Billy was only wearing his usual too small neon shorts and a red t-shirt cut off below his pecs.

"I swear when I moved to Hollywood I didn't expect anything like this," I gestured toward the porn producer who was on his knees trying to coax Kitty Purry from under the couch. Chris's face was like stone, and I had to look away. Finally Kitty Purry came out and Billy scooped her up and grinned at us.

"Sorry, she's at that special age. In a matter of months I probably won't be able to wake her up except to feed her." He held her tight against his chest with one arm, and with his other hand he fished a set of keys out of his pockets. "I'm leaving in a few days, and I had this set of keys made for you guys."

Chris held his hand out and Billy dropped them into his palm. "You guys look like you're in the middle of something. Sorry I interrupted." A shadow passed over Billy's face, and he slowly walked to the door.

"It's nothing, Billy." I said, following along behind him.

Chris frowned, and I realized it wasn't nothing to him. Fuck it, I had to get out of here before I said something else wrong. "I was just heading out for a little fresh air."

When I jogged past Chris, I noticed his pursed lips trembling. This wasn't going to work. How on earth were we supposed to live together with this heavy shit hanging between us?

I raced to the elevator. When I glanced back down the hall, Chris, Billy, and the kitten were staring at me like I was crazy.

Chris's eyes fell to the floor, then he turned and walked into the apartment without saying another word.

My chest tightened as the elevator doors shut behind me, and suddenly it all became too much. Tears spilled down my cheeks, and I slumped against the back wall of the elevator. Damn it, why did this have to happen now?

CHAPTER 18

CHRIS- ONE WEEK LATER

"Would you like something to drink while you wait, Mr. Reynolds?" Marla's receptionist asked. I shook my head no, then shut my eyes. Since Jett shot me down, I hadn't been sleeping well, so every chance I got was spent trying to rest so I wouldn't look so haggard during photo shoots and auditions.

Marla asked me to her office so she could tell me some news. It was probably to fire me as a client. I'd auditioned with Hugo for a part in his latest movie, and I could barely remember how it went. All I recalled was the part was for his character's best friend, who was desperate to get Hugo's character to lay off drugs. I practically mumbled my way through the audition, so I was sure I hadn't got the part.

"Mr. Reynolds?"

My eyes popped open. "Did I fall asleep?"

"No, sweetie. Ms. Fleming will see you now."

I stood and walked into Marla's office. When I shut the door behind me, Marla gestured to the chair opposite hers and I sat down. She looked at me with an expression that made my stomach lurch. This was it—she was going to let me go.

"So," she said, her voice soft yet firm. "I have some news for you."

I nodded, bracing myself for the worst.

Marla took a deep breath, then smiled. "The casting director for *Bad Habits* was thrilled with your audition." Marla's eyes twinkled and I felt my heart skip a beat. "The part of Kevin Graham, who plays Hugo's best friend? It's yours if you want it."

I rose from the chair, almost too stunned to move. "What?!" I asked, disbelief in my voice. "I thought I did awful, like I was sleepwalking through the scene." Marla waved her hand for me to sit again. "No, that was exactly what the casting director wanted. You had to portray the fact that your character couldn't help Hugo's character without becoming overly sentimental or melodramatic. Whatever you did, it definitely worked."

"Wow," I mumbled, then sat down. "I'm actually going to be in a movie."

Marla smiled. "You certainly are." She grabbed a folder from her desk and handed it to me. It was a copy of the contract she'd negotiated with the studio on my behalf. "It's your first film, so the pay isn't stellar, but it's definitely enough for you to lay off the modeling gigs. And if the film is a hit, which I know it will be, the sky's the limit."

She pressed a button on her phone and spoke. "Gloria, make sure to get the press releases out for Hugo and Chris's next movie this morning."

"So what happens next?" I asked.

"I'm booking you some interviews over the next few weeks. Where are you from again?" She began typing on her desktop computer.

"Richmond, Virginia."

"Okay, I'll be sure to book interviews with the local markets there and in Washington DC." She typed for a few more seconds than focused on me again. "So, do you remember our conversation at Becks and Hugo's house? By the pool?"

It took me a second, then I slowly nodded. I hoped she didn't want to talk about that. It wasn't like Jett and I ended up together. If anything, the conversation had driven a wedge between us. Now whenever we saw each other, we'd come up with excuses to go to our respective bedrooms alone.

"You know, the two of you look perfect together." She steepled her hands under her chin. "Jett's playing his first live gig in California in two days. Has he told you about it?"

I shrugged. "Not really."

"It's at Catch One, the biggest LGBTQ concert venue in Los Angeles." She stood, walked over to the mini-fridge and pulled out two bottles of water, handing me one before she took her seat. "His producer Clint is amazing, and thanks to Jett having recorded so many songs independently, all Clint had to do was polish up enough songs for a set. They've also recorded a couple of new tracks, and one of them releases the day of the show. The week after that, Jett will be on tour for a couple of weeks, doing shows in San Francisco, Santa Barbara, Palm Springs."

"Okay, great," I shook my head noncommittally.

"Why aren't you acting more enthusiastically?" Marla tilted her head. "I thought you two were dating?"

My eyes dropped to my lap.

"Oh my God." Marla's eyes rolled. "You two are perfect together. And the publicity would be fabulous."

"He's not interested in me," I murmured. "Jett says he must focus on his career right now, and it's a bad time for rela-tionships."

"What the actual hell?" Marla bit her lower lip. "You know,

as his agent, I love his dedication. But as a friend of both of yours, this really sucks."

I nodded again, understanding full well how she felt, but unable to offer any reassurances or solutions at this point either. We sat in silence for a few moments before Marla spoke up again with a devilish smile on her lips.

"If he won't see what he's missing, then maybe you should show him." She suggested mischievously, before adding: "That show at Catch One is gonna be huge – it'll be the perfect place for you two to reconnect."

"We fucking live together Marla." Good God, was my agent becoming a matchmaker too? "Every time we see each other we turn around and go in opposite directions. To be honest, I wouldn't be surprised if he moved out soon. He's making enough money to afford a nice place on his own." My tone dropped. "I hate the tension between us. If he moved out, we might be able to be friends again after enough time has passed."

Marla came around her desk, stood behind me, and began squeezing my shoulders. "I understand if you're hurt, but is there any way you can at least try to be friends now? Obviously I can't force you two to date, but you guys look so awesome together. It's much easier to promote two up-and-coming talents who hang out socially. Jett hates the PR side of things, and I really need him to get on board with promoting his work. With you around, it might make him more comfortable."

I choked out a laugh. "Trust me, Marla, Jett's not relaxed when I'm around. All I do is make him hide in his room, or take long, midnight strolls to avoid the apartment."

Marla sighed, her hands still rubbing circles on my shoulders. "I guess Jett needs space right now," she said. "But perhaps he needs a little nudge in the right direction. You're going to be my date at Catch One for his show, and Hugo and Becks are coming too. Wear something sexy. It'll be a great opportunity for you to show Jett what he's missing out on, plus it's great PR for everybody."

Marla walked back to her side of the desk and winked at me, obviously pleased with herself and her idea. I smiled back weakly, knowing it was probably a lost cause, but still feeling somewhat hopeful that maybe something could come from her plan.

———

When I arrived back at the apartment, I saw the light on in Jett's window from the sidewalk. "I hope he fed Kitty Purry," I muttered, then kept on walking. It had been like this ever since he told me how he really felt. Being in the apartment with him was stressful, with so many unspoken feelings twisting inside me.

As for what he thought about the situation, I wasn't a mind reader. He might be totally cool with how things worked out. I had no way of knowing.

A few minutes later Flaming Saddles came into view, so I ducked in for a drink. This was one place I knew Jett wouldn't go to, so it was safe for me to hang out there for a little while.

The front of the bar was packed as usual, so I headed toward the back where the mechanical bull was located. Why they had such a thing, I didn't know since I'd never seen anyone riding it.

"What can I get for ya, cowboy," A waiter wearing the tacky uniform asked me. Then he did a double take, and asked, "Aren't you friends with Jett Sumner? Oh, and Hugo Zepeda and Becket Grant?"

There went my privacy. I guess this was just a taste of what to expect after I made the movie with Hugo. Hell, shouldn't I be just a little more excited about that?

"Yeah, we're buddies." I muttered. "Just bring me whatever's on tap."

The waiter nodded and brought back my beer as I settled into a booth. My eyes wandered around the room as people laughed, talked, flirted and drank. I wished Jett was here instead of avoiding me like the plague.

I drained half the mug, then noticed the waiter still staring at me from across the room. Not wanting to encourage him to come over and talk, I began scrolling on my phone.

"Oh, wow." My eyes widened as I checked Google Alerts. Marla wasted no time issuing the press release about me and Hugo starring in *Bad Habits*. Of course, the gossip sites were going crazy about my Golden Globe winning best friend. But hell, at least they were mentioning me in the same sentence as Hugo.

There were several text messages from friends and family, all wishing me luck. I was about to call my parents when the waiter came back.

"Hey, I'm sorry to bother you," The waiter sat across from me. I shrugged and placed the phone on the table. "My name is Cam, and when I'm not here, I book musical acts around town. What's going on with Jett? There are all these industry reports about him working with Clint Cash. Then I saw he was booked at Catch One, and I contacted his agent to see if she'd allow me to book him at The Scorpio Room. The bitch was rude as hell, told me he was bigger than that and hung up on me."

Good 'ol Marla.

"We actually share an agent. She probably wasn't being rude on purpose," I crossed my fingers under the table. Hopefully he couldn't tell I was lying. "He scored a record deal, and after the show at Catch One, he's going on tour. That's why he quit working here."

"If the money wasn't so good, I'd quit too." The waiter stood, then placed a hand on my shoulder. "You know, if you ever want to meet for coffee or something..."

If Jett hadn't walked back into my life, I'd probably say yes. The guy seemed nice enough, and he was definitely easy on the eyes. But now I was suspicious. Was he asking me out because I was friends with famous people, or was he genuinely interested? Hell, it didn't matter, because until I got over Jett, I'd be incredibly bad company.

"Thanks, but..."

"Don't worry, dude. I understand." The waiter backed away from the table and smiled. "Let me get you another beer, and this one's on me."

CHAPTER 19

JETT

walked up the steps of Pineapple Dance Studios, my heart
pounding in my chest. Every time I came to the studio I
thought I'd have a panic attack. No matter what Tonia tried
to teach me, I still had two left feet. Thank goodness I had
backup dancers and a singer to take some of the focus off of me.

Sweat poured down my sides from nerves, and I still hadn't
set foot inside. Was this stage fright? Or just terror knowing
that tomorrow night I was performing at Catch One. If it was
just an ordinary performance like the ones I'd done on the East
Coast, I wouldn't be so freaked out. But now the record
company was recording the performance to release on social
media. There were also going to be numerous industry types
and reporters there. I wanted to entertain fans, not a bunch of
music bigwigs in suits.

I closed my eyes and took a deep breath. "It'll be okay," I
whispered, though it didn't feel true at all as another wave of
anxiety washed through me. Then something Tonia said came
unbidden to mind - "It's not about perfection - it's about putting
your heart and soul into every move."

"Since I can't dance, I'd better be prepared to sing my ass off," I mumbled, then opened the door.

"Hi, Jett," Portia Camino waved to me from a couch in the reception area. I smiled at her, amazed as always by how beautiful she was. She was a classic Italian beauty with olive skin and dark eyes, and her voice was one of the best I'd ever heard. She was a total pro, and pulled no punches helping me perfect my own performance.

"Please, tell me they've canceled the concert." I sat next to her and laid my head on her shoulder.

"Fuck no, I need to get paid, bitch." She laughed. "Gurl, we're going to rock that show. Stop stressing about it. Neither of us can dance, but we have the voices. Let the backup dancers do their thing, and we'll do ours."

Portia's words of encouragement were just what I needed. I sat up straighter and nodded my head.

"You're right," I inhaled. "Let's do this."

The door to the studio opened and Charlie C. strolled into the reception area, his golden skin covered with sweat. He and his boyfriend, Timothy X. were the backup dancers, and were rehearsing quite a bit more than me and Portia. "Oh good, Tonia's ready for the four of us to work together."

"C'mon, you've got this." Portia stood, held out her hand, and pulled me to my feet. "Trust your voice." She grabbed her throat and pointed at me. "That's why people pay to see you." Portia took my hand and dragged me into the studio.

"Amori miei, benvenuti!" Tonia smiled as we walked in. It was Italian, I thought. I'd grown to appreciate the choreographer and dance teacher over the last few days. I was a horrible dancer, but somehow she'd taught me enough to move around on a stage without peeing my pants.

"Hi, Jett."

I turned toward the voice and saw Marla and some plain-looking dude in a suit seated on a bench. Damn it, now I felt even more pressure. Marla waved for me to come over, so I laid my jacket next to Portia's and approached them.

"Jett, this is Samuel Farmer. He works A&R for the record label." Marla gestured toward the man who stood up to shake my hand. He looked like the starched-shirt type of executive I'd come to expect from most corporate jobs. He probably had to wear a tie every day just to have a backbone.

"Nice to meet you," I muttered, then turned to Marla. "I didn't know I had an audience for this rehearsal."

"We need to make sure we recoup our investment with you." The man said curtly, then sat down and began typing on his phone. Marla took my arm and dragged me across the room.

"Play nice with the record company, Jett," Marla hissed. "The other reason I'm here is to let you know that Chris is my date for your show."

"What?" My eyebrows shot up.

"I didn't want you to see him in the audience and freak out." She whispered. "He got a part in Hugo's next movie, *Bad Habits,* and he needs the publicity. Hugo and Becks will be there too. Didn't Chris tell you about it? I mean, you two are roommates."

"No," I sighed, guilt spreading through my limbs. "We're not really hanging out right now."

"Everyone, take your places." Tonia clapped her hands. "Here are your microphones."

I strolled over and took one of them, and Portia took the other.

"We've got this," Portia winked.

I swallowed hard and tried to compose myself while Tonia barked directions at Charlie and Timothy in the middle of the room. Damn it, now all I could think about was Chris, and how shitty our living situation had become. We'd literally not spoken more than two or three sentences since I told him I wasn't interested in dating. Now I wondered if I'd made a mistake. For fuck's sake, he'd gotten a role in a major motion picture and he hadn't told me?

"God damn it," I mumbled, and Portia gave me the side eye.

"Places everyone!" Tonia barked. Portia and I moved to the center of the room, and Timothy and Charlie stood behind us. Then she switched on the tape of the first track, and beats filled the room.

When I stepped forward for the first part of the dance sequence, I thought I'd throw up. Portia grabbed my arm, pulled me forward, then sang the opening line.

"First, last, only one baby." Her voice was incredible, rich and smooth. I forced a smile on my face, a singer's trick to prevent my voice from sounding flat. Then I began to sing.

I've been looking for my heart's desire,
A love that feels like home.
I've searched high and low, far and wide,
But I always feel alone.

I found my rhythm, following Portia's lead as we danced the simple routine Tonia taught us. Our choreographer clapped to the beat, occasionally shouting directions to Timothy and Charlie, whose routine was much more detailed.

But then I saw him at the club one night,
My heart skipped a beat.
I knew right then and there,
He's the one, the only one.

Portia spun around, threw her arms out in front of her, and I spun around too. Then I held my mike out and we sang the chorus together through the same microphone.

He's the only one I want to love,
The only one I want to dance with.
He's the only one I want to hold,

The only one I want to be with.

I glanced over to Marla and the record company suit, and both were grinning ear to ear while tapping their feet. Thank God.

We made it through the entire song without any hiccups—I even managed to stay on beat for most of it—and when we finished Tonia gave us all thumbs up.

"That was great!" She said with a huge smile on her face. "Now let's take it from the top again."

————

"I'll take you home," Marla said, "or anywhere you want. We need to talk."

"Give me a sec, I want to put my normal clothes on."

The glittery costume I'd worn to rehearsal was drenched with sweat, so I ran to the bathroom and changed into a pair of jeans and a t-shirt I kept in my backpack. The costume would be cleaned and pressed by tomorrow night.

I knew what she wanted to talk about, or rather, who. When I stepped back into the reception area, she took my arm and dragged me out of the dance studio. Jesus, my agent acted more like my boss than someone I employed.

"New car?" I pointed at the shiny white Mercedes. Marla nodded, unlocked the doors with her keyfob, and I slid into the front seat. It had that new car smell coupled with the scent of vanilla or chocolate. She switched on the ignition, and you could barely hear the engine.

"I know this isn't any of my business, but Chris isn't handling things very well." She backed out of the parking spot using the computer screen on the dashboard as a guide.

"You're right, it's not." I crossed my arms over my chest. "You're my agent, not my mother." Though my mother would never have brought up anything about my love life. As far as she was concerned I was a virgin.

"I know, I know." She pulled out of the parking lot onto Sunset Boulevard. "But I would like to think we're friends, too."

A blue pickup truck cut her off, and she slammed on the horn. "Watch where you're going fuck face!"

"Marla..."

"Sorry, my anger management issues always come out when I'm behind the wheel. My therapist says I have control issues." Marla turned in her seat, angling away from the road to see me. Her hands gripped the steering wheel with white knuckles.

"Duh," I chuckled, and she laughed.

"About Chris, he's..."

"Marla, I appreciate that you care, but this is really personal. Does Chris know you're talking to me about him?" I tilted my head.

"Of course not." She sniffed. "Look, Chris told me you don't want to date anyone with all the chaos surrounding your career right now. As your agent, I appreciate the dedication. Oh, and by the way, you can dance! I saw you dancing and singing at the studio and you were fucking fantastic." She hooked her thumb toward the back seat. "Grab my purse. I need a hit of nicotine gum."

I pulled the black and white Chanel bag onto my lap and opened it. The pack of gum was on top, so I fished a piece out and handed it to her.

"Thanks." She popped it in her mouth and sighed. A moment later she took a deep breath and began to speak slowly as if I were a child. "Both you and Chris are going through a lot of changes. He's got a juicy supporting role in Hugo's movie, and if it's a hit, his life will never be the same again. You're also on the cusp of success. Haven't you ever thought that maybe it would be easier on both of you if you had each other for support?"

I let her words sink in.

"Chris is so sweet, and good God, he's a fucking model. How can you say no to him? If I were in your shoes I'd jump on him every chance I could and ride him like a pogo stick." Marla flipped the turn signal, and turned onto my street.

"Who says I haven't done precisely that already?" I smirked, then the ball of nerves in my stomach began to twist around.

"Oh, you two have already, shit, that's none of my business." Marla shook her head, then pulled into the parking lot of my building. "Look, I just want my two favorite guys to be happy. You can be there for each other while your lives go through this transformation together. Trust me, I know the toll stardom can take on people. That's why Hugo's the actor, not me. I had to deal with my parents freaking out all the time. No way I'd ever want that life."

She freaked out all the time, and it had nothing to do with being an actor.

"Marla, I've been giving it a lot of thought, and maybe I was wrong." I shut my eyes for a moment, pondering what she'd just said. The idea of having someone to rely on when the going got tough was appealing, plus I couldn't stop thinking about Chris. Night and day, he was living rent free inside my head, and my heart. I felt her hand on my arm, and opened my eyes. She was pointing toward the entrance to my building.

"Shit." I whispered. Chris was walking up the steps, and apparently hadn't seen us. Damn, he must have been at the gym. His skin was glistening, and he was wearing a pair of shorts and a sweat-soaked t-shirt that clung to his tan skin.

Marla leaned into me and whispered, "Maybe this is your chance to make things right?"

CHAPTER 20

CHRIS

W hen I got to the front door of my apartment building, I felt like I was being watched. It was unnerving, and by the time I made it to my apartment, the feeling had only grown.

I hadn't seen any signs that Jett was here, so instead of racing to my room, I went to the kitchen and slugged back an entire liter of cold water. Hugo introduced me to his personal trainer so I could be in the best shape possible before filming began, and the workouts were excruciating. I refilled the water bottle and put it in the freezer, then I heard the sound of the front door opening.

"Shit," I whispered. This meant another wordless greeting, the cold shoulder, and a game of who could stay in their room the longest before the other guy left.

"Hey," Jett filled the kitchen doorway. "Can we talk?"

My pulse picked up. This could go in several directions. We could argue, but I doubted that. Neither of us liked confrontations. Or, we could politely converse about the weather and race back to our respective bedrooms. Worst case scenario?

He'd tell me he was moving out, and we'd have an awkward conversation involving the words, "It's me, not you." Which everyone knew was utter bullshit.

"Sure," I shrugged, grabbed another cold bottle of water out of the fridge, and followed Jett into the living room.

We sat down and Jett began, "So. How's it been going?"

I took a deep breath. We both knew why we were here, but neither of us wanted to say it out loud. We'd been avoiding each other for weeks now and I wasn't sure if he was waiting for an apology or what. He didn't look mad, though; he looked sad.

"It's been tough," I admitted softly. "But good things have happened too."

"Marla told me all about your upcoming movie, and Mom texted me about it too. She said there was an interview with you in Style Weekly back home." Jett crossed his legs, then uncrossed them.

"Yeah, Marla stuck me in a broom closet in her office with a phone and I spoke to reporters for a few hours. Mostly the small papers in Virginia and DC." I unscrewed the water bottle and took a long sip. "She had a script prepared for me so I wouldn't say anything stupid."

Jett chuckled. "She's a bit of a control freak, but she gets the job done. Are you handling things okay?"

I sighed and looked down at my hands. I knew what he was asking and it felt like a huge weight on my chest. We'd been avoiding each other for weeks now and I wasn't sure if he wanted an apology or what. But I had to try and make things right between us.

"Look, I'm sorry things have been uncomfortable between us." I realized my leg was jumping up and down so I laid my hand on my thigh to calm it. "I shouldn't have put you on the spot about wanting to date you."

"Stop," Jett held his hand up. "You said nothing wrong. I'm terrified of how my life is about to change. According to Marla, you're going through the same kind of stuff. She also made a good point."

"What's that?"

"That maybe it would be better if we had each other while going through all these changes." Jett's face turned pink. "I mean, maybe we should… try dating." His voice was low and he wouldn't meet my eyes.

Jesus, neither of us was really good with emotions. Why was it so hard to say what we really felt? Was it how we were raised to be men? Out of touch with our emotions, or was it just being human, scared of rejection?

Finally, I managed to stammer out, "Y-yeah, uh… sure." I could feel my cheeks burning as an embarrassed smile tugged at the corners of my mouth. Jett crossed the room and sat beside me on the couch. He reached out and grabbed my hand, before saying, "Can I take you out on a real date then? Maybe something fancy? Of course, it will have to be in a few weeks, after I get back from the tour."

"Shooting for *Bad Habits* starts in three weeks, so that means we probably don't have a lot of time for… you know what? Who gives a damn about a real date! When I'm with you, I have fun, we laugh, and you know, we don't have to be so formal." I picked up Jett's hand, turned it over and kissed his palm. Out of the corner of my eye I saw two short white sticks on the table that hadn't been there before. I must have made a face, because Jett tilted his head, then followed my gaze.

"Are those cigarettes?" I nodded toward the coffee table. "Isn't it bad for singers to smoke?"

"Oh, no, no." Jett snatched one of them up. "Clint, my producer, keeps giving me weed after our recording sessions. He says I need to loosen up. I've never smoked it before, so I've been giving them to my dancers. For some reason I thought I'd give it a try, so I kept these two for myself."

"You've smoked weed before." I giggled, surprised he didn't remember. "When we were at Steward School in the ninth grade, you, me, and William Florman skipped school one day. We walked through the trails behind the Whitaker Woods neighborhood and William lit up a joint. Neither of us had smoked before, so we both took little puffs and William was pissed because we were wasting good weed. It didn't do anything for me."

"Why don't I remember that?" Jett held the joint under his nose. "I kinda like the way it smells."

I took the joint from him and laid it on the table. "I want to kiss you, and I'd prefer it if we both have our wits about us."

Jett's eyes widened with surprise and his mouth opened in a soft O.

"K-kiss?" he stammered.

I smiled and nodded, moving closer to him on the couch. "If you don't want to, I understand. Take all the time you need to..."

Jett laid his index finger over my lips, then brushed his lips across my cheek. "Of course I want to kiss you," he breathed. His eyes locked on mine, and a moment later he removed his finger and replaced it with his lips. The kiss was gentle and slow. Jett's lips were warm, and his mouth tasted like coffee and mints. Utterly delicious.The low thud of my heartbeat pulsed in my ears. Jett's hands grabbed my head, pinning me in place, and his fingertips raked across my scalp. *This is what I want, what I've wanted since Jett moved in.* This feeling of being as one with him, and I never wanted it to end. Suddenly, Jett pulled away, and I groaned with frustration.

"Did you hear that?" He panted.

"No," I reached for his shoulders, and he pulled back.

"Maybe I do need to unwind." Jett gave me a tight smile, then picked up one of the joints. "Do you have a lighter?"

"Are you sure?" I cocked an eyebrow. Jett shrugged and nodded yes.

"Back in a minute." I strolled into the kitchen, opened up the drawer filled with Hugo's cooking stuff, and found what appeared to be a mini blow torch. I clicked the black button and a jet of fire came out the other end. "This should work."

When I returned, Jett had an odd look on his face.

"I swear I keep hearing something jumping around." Jett swiveled his head around the room.

"Are you sure you want to smoke this?" I sat next to him and pulled the joint out of his fingers. "It might make you paranoid." He already seemed that way, but I didn't want to point that out.

"No, I need to start doing things differently." Jett gestured for me to light up. "And if this can help me relax, why not? Plus, it's legal. They say it's safer than booze."

I lit the joint with the mini-blow torch, inhaled, then passed it to Jett. He took a long hit from it, and attempted to hold it in. Instead, he coughed most of the smoke out.

"Yuck," He scrunched up his face, then took another hit from it. This time he held the smoke in without coughing. Jett passed it back to me, then blew the smoke in my face. It was my turn to cough. I rarely smoked weed, or anything else. Occasionally I'd pick up an edible at a dispensary, but that was the extent of my drug use. When I stubbed the joint out in the never used antique ashtray Hugo left behind, Jett put his arms around me and pulled me in for another kiss.

Jett's lips found mine, and I was swept away with emotion. My arms encircled him, then he pulled back. Jett's eyes darted around the room, and his eyebrows drew together. "Why do I keep hearing that weird noise?"

"I don't hear anything."

"Why can't you hear that?" Jett stood and started pacing around the apartment. When he got to the front door, he stopped and pressed his ear to it. "It's Kitty Purry. Can't you hear her crying?"

Kitty Purry was meowing from Billy's apartment across the hall. Jett muttered, "I forgot to feed her this morning. Did you do it?"

"Damn it, I forgot too." My shoulders slumped. Cock blocked by a kitten. The meows grew louder.

Jett grabbed his keys off the coffee table. "Come on, we'll go take care of Kitty Purry, then come back here and finish what we started."

I stood up, grabbed him by the waist and nuzzled his neck. "You promise?"

"Promise," Jett murmured, then kissed the tip of my nose. "C'mon, let's get this over with." He took my hand and led me to the door. When he opened it, a loud crash echoed from Billy's apartment.

"What the hell was that?"

CHAPTER 21
CHRIS

ett crossed the hallway and stuck his key in the lock. When he opened the door, Kitty Purry's little meow sounded muted, like she was under something. "Where is she?"

"Oh shit, look!" I pointed at the far wall. The camera set up Billy used for filming porn had fallen over. "Oh my God, I hope Kitty is okay." I walked over to the fallen equipment and picked it up, placing the camera against the wall. Then I felt something furry brushing against my lower leg.

"There she is." Jett scooped up the fluffy black kitten and held her against his cheek. "She probably tried to climb it. Don't scare us like that again Kitty Purry."

"Meow."

A goofy grin spread across Jett's cheeks, and his eyes were now glazed pink. "She's so adorable."

Jett was the adorable one, though Kitty Purry was a close second. "I'll open a can of food, then we can get back to what we were doing." I waggled my eyebrows, and felt dizzy. Jett winked at me. When I turned to go to Billy's kitchen, I stepped on a tiny stuffed mouse and nearly fell over. "Shit." I righted myself, and stumbled into the kitchen.

"Where the hell is the cat food again?" I searched the cabinets, and finally found Kitty's food stacked in neat little rows under the sink. Grabbing a saucer out of the dish drain, I opened the can and immediately heard little feet running. She didn't even give me a chance to put the food in the dish. Kitty scrambled up my legs, and when she got to my back her little claws dug into my skin through my t-shirt.

"Ouch!" I gasped, trying to suppress a laugh as Jett came running into the kitchen.

"What's going on?" He asked, his eyes wide with worry.

I pointed to Kitty on my back while gasping for breath in between fits of laughter. Jett gently took Kitty off of me and set her down on the ground. After spooning food into the saucer he put it on the floor next to her. She nearly bit his fingers off trying to get to the saucer.

"Be a good girl," he said sternly before reaching over and giving me a kiss on the forehead. "Are you okay?"

I nodded, still laughing as I tried to catch my breath. "Yeah, just some very sharp kitty claws."

"While you were in here, I well, couldn't help but look at some of Billy's stuff." Jett grabbed my hand and dragged me back to the living room. The wooden cabinet where Billy kept his sex toys, condoms, lube, and other props for his movies was wide open.

"Are you sure we should be going through his stuff?" I asked, then Jett let go of my hand and grabbed an odd-looking white contraption off the shelf.

"What the hell is this?"

"It looks like a modem, except a little bigger." I took it from him. There were several buttons on it, and across the top was the word AUTOBLOW. Turning it over, I saw a hole in the bottom and knew exactly what it was for. "Oh, this is um, you know," My face felt like it was on fire. "Blowjobs."

"Huh?" Jett took it back from me and examined it. "I thought Billy was into giving blowjobs. Wouldn't this take away all his fun?"

"He's into anything. What I don't understand is why any guy would want to stick his dick in there. Like, it's plastic." I put it back on the shelf and scanned the other devices. "I prefer the real deal, know what I mean?" I turned and winked at Jett. "Now this is truly strange." I picked up a small pink fluffy thing. "Oh, it's a butt plug with a pink bunny tail."

"Oh, I bet that photographs well." Jett murmured, and I realized he'd officially been in Hollywood too long. Anyone in the business of being photographed often would immediately think that. "Now this one baffles me." Jett picked up what appeared to be a leather belt with bright red silicone lips. "What on earth is this?"

"It's a ball gag, I think."

"What?" Jett giggled. "How do you gag balls?"

"Give that to me," I took it from him. "Okay, let me unbuckle the leather thingy." After I got that done, I positioned it in front of my mouth. Underneath the red lips was where you put your teeth. Without thinking I did it, then gestured for Jett to buckle the thing. I prayed that filthy Billy had sanitized it.

"What are you doing, is this like gay charades?" Jett tilted his head. I pointed at the buckle while making odd noises since my lips couldn't move. "Oh!" Jett stepped behind me and buckled it up. Then he backed away, held his sides, and began to cackle.

"You, you, can't shut your mouth!" He chortled. A moment later he fell back against the couch, slapping the cushions. "Like, you stick your dick in there and..."

I reached behind my head and fumbled with the buckle.

When I got it off I laid on top of him. "You don't need anything to hold my mouth open, trust me." I felt his cock firming up underneath me. "Toys are fun, I guess. I don't have a lot of experience with them. The human touch is what I crave."

Jett shut his eyes and pushed his hips up against my erection. I moaned, "Your touch, Chris. That's what I want."

My lips crashed into his, and all thoughts of sex toys flew out of my head. I kissed him with every ounce of longing in my body. Jett responded in kind as his hands roamed my back and chest. We rolled around on the couch, greedy for each other's touch. I grabbed the hem of Jett's shirt and pulled it up over his head, only breaking the kiss for a split second. His chest was smooth and pale and I ran my hands over it, feeling the heat radiating off him. He moaned into my mouth, pushing against me as his arousal grew more intense.

Jett's hands moved down to unbutton my jeans while mine slid inside his pants, exploring every inch of him with fervor. He gasped as I massaged his shaft through the fabric of his underwear.

"Too many clothes," I breathed. My lips trailed down from his mouth along his neck, then lower to find his nipples hardening at the touch of my tongue. When I reached them, Jett let out a moan that vibrated through us both as he thrust his cock against me.

"Jett," I glanced up at his face contorted with pleasure. "Too many fucking clothes."

I moved down his body until my lips hovered over his cock, still encased in his pants. I unbuttoned them, then pulled them all the way off. Then I unzipped my jeans, yanked them down and nearly fell over. When I lay down on top of him again, he flipped me over and climbed on top of me. He nibbled my lower lip before dipping his tongue inside my mouth. Jett tasted like warm spiced wine with a hint of mint, and every time his hips pushed down against mine he moaned into my mouth.

"I want more," Jett muttered, breaking the kiss. His lips worked their way down my neck to my chest. He lifted my arm, then kissed the tender skin beneath my armpit.

"Ah..." I groaned, then he nibbled his way down my side. When he got to my hip he stopped, gripped my cock at the base, and placed the head of my dick in his mouth.

"Yes," my back arched, and Jett began swirling his tongue around the head while pulling on the base of my dick. Seriously Jett knew how to suck cock, like, he only needed a few moments of licking and pulling and I could feel an orgasm starting to build. Then he let go of my shaft, pushed my legs up, and began licking underneath my balls. When I felt his fingers sliding over my entrance, I froze.

Jett stopped, looked up at me and smiled. "I want more, you know. Like, let's take this to the next level."

"Um, yeah, about that." I motioned for him to move up. A second later he was flat against my body, his rock hard cock pressing against mine. "I've never done that before."

"You mean with me, right?" He brushed his lips across my cheeks.

"No, I've never done it with anyone." Jett and I had always had oral sex, and I'd never met a guy that inspired me to go any further. "I guess I'm a virgin."

"So am I," Jett's cheeks pinkened. "And you're the only guy I've ever considered doing it with."

"You mean fucking, right?" I winked, and a giggling fit overcame both of us. Deep down inside we were both shy preppy boys from Richmond, trying to become stars in decadent Hollywood. Jett kissed me again, then stood up, his hard cock pointing at his belly button. He held his hand out, then pulled me to my feet. "Let's go back to our place, this is..." He looked confused for a moment, then pointed behind me. I turned, and sitting on top of the sofa was a very curious kitten staring at us.

"Do you think Kitty's been watching the whole time?" I whispered, as if she could understand us. "Oh listen, she's purring." I stroked the side of her face.

"We definitely can't do anything else here." Jett walked over to the sex-toy cabinet, grabbed an enormous bottle of lube and jogged to the door. "Get our clothes."

I scooped them up, and realized I didn't have any condoms. Since Jett was a virgin too, I guessed he didn't have any either. There was a goldfish bowl full of them next to a dildo shaped like a traffic cone. I grabbed a few, then Jett slowly opened the door and peered down the hallway. Can't let the neighbors catch us now, can we?

"The coast is clear," he whispered. "Let's go!"

CHAPTER 22
JETT

After making sure the coast was clear I dashed across the hall to our apartment. Chris followed behind me, and as soon as he shut our door, we both heard a door open, then shut. Chris whispered, "That was close."

We stood there silently for a moment, as if the neighbor could hear us. Footsteps padded down the hallway, and a moment later the soft bell of the elevator rang out. Perhaps we should have gotten dressed before crossing the hallway? *Nah. That wouldn't be fun.*

"Did you remember to shut Billy's door?" I whispered, visions of Kitty Purry escaping the building filled my brain.

"Yes," Chris replied. "And why are we whispering?"

Nerves. That was why I was doing it. It felt like we were eighteen again, sneaking around behind our parents' backs. Stolen moments in the back of Chris's hand-me-down ancient Volvo were permanently etched in my brain. The biggest difference now was that we didn't have to hide any more.

Chris grabbed my hand and pulled me closer to him, his

eyes burning with desire. He ran his finger down my arm, sending a shiver up my spine.

"I want you now more than I ever have before," he murmured, his voice low and a deep hunger in his expression.

My heart raced as I took in the sight of him, standing there with nothing on. His muscular chest and strong arms were tantalizingly close, and I needed to touch him. My body ached for him, in a different way than I'd desired in the past. When we had sex in the past, it was more like fooling around. Now I wanted to make love.

Chris dropped his clothes on the floor, including several brightly colored condoms. He leaned over and snatched them up before straightening back up again. He grinned mischievously at me and asked, "Your room or mine?"

My mind went blank for a moment. Oh, yeah, we each had a room. Was this the weed clouding my brain, or was it the sight of Chris standing naked in front of me?

Yours," I answered as my pulse raced faster at the thought of what we were about to do. Chris nodded, then grabbed my hand again before leading me into his bedroom. He dimmed the lights and lit some candles on the dresser.

"I'll take that," Chris grabbed the jug of lube from my arms and placed it on the nightstand, dropping the condoms next to it.

The warm light of the candles flooded the room, giving it a romantic ambiance. I felt my pulse ramp up as Chris leaned in and kissed me. His hands roamed up and down from my neck to my ass while his lips worked their magic. He abruptly let go of me and stood back, his eyes traveling up and down my frame. The intensity of his gaze sent a thrill through me, and I stepped into his arms for another kiss.

His hands cupped my ass, and he began walking us backward until my legs hit his bed and I fell back on it. Once again he stared at me, naked and vulnerable on his bed. Part of me wanted to cover myself, but the other part wanted to open myself to him completely. When we first talked about fucking, I'd thought I would be the top, or giver, or whatever they called it. Now I wanted to know what it would be like to make myself vulnerable in the most intimate way possible to Chris.

"Kiss me," I whispered.

Chris lay down on top of me and obliged, his lips gentle and sweet as they explored mine. His hands roamed up and down my body, creating a trail of fire wherever they touched. He moved them to my chest and caressed my nipples until they hardened under his touch. I gasped at the sensation, arching my back and pressing myself closer to him.

Chris's lips left mine, licking his way down my neck to my nipples, tracing circles around the hard nubs. He took one of them between his teeth, confusing my body with feelings of both pleasure and pain. Then he continued licking his way down my stomach, causing me to gasp. When he reached my cock, he flicked his tongue over the sensitive area under the head, and my hands grasped the sides of his head, hoping for more.

Chris took my cock in his mouth, and my eyes snapped shut. I was so close already, and didn't want this to end yet. He only used his mouth and tongue, and that wonderful pressure began to build under my groin. Then I felt his fingers against my entrance, and instead of being surprised, I wanted to feel more of him inside of me.

My cock fell out of his mouth for a moment. I opened my eyes and he had his middle and index fingers in his mouth. A moment later he rubbed my hole again, and I could feel his slick fingers teasing me.

"Please," I moaned. "I want to feel what it's like."

With my cock back in his mouth he inched a finger inside of

me. I'd done this to myself before, and had always wondered what all the fuss was about concerning backdoor activities. But then he stuck the second finger inside of me and hit something.

"Oh my God." It felt like every pleasure point in my body was activated at once, like a giant wave. Chris began moving his fingers in and out of me, and every time he touched that spot it was like electricity shooting up my spine, straight to my brain. "Chris, I'm ready, I need more."

He slowly withdrew his fingers, then gazed down at my cock.

"Wow," Chris murmured, grasping my dick. I glanced down and saw a stream of precome flowing down my shaft. He leaned down, took my cock in his mouth, and I nearly exploded.

"Please, I need you inside of me now, Chris." I panted.

He moved up my body and kissed me, hard. I tasted my juices on his lips, and my hips bucked. Chris reached over for the lube and pumped a handful into his palm, then carefully rubbed it into my entrance. Then he rubbed the rest over my cock and reached for a condom. Chris ripped the package open with his teeth then rolled it down his length. He eyed me, and I detected a hint of nerves.

"I want yout so bad, Jett," He murmured, placing my knees over his shoulders. "But this is my first time, so I might not be very…"

"Trust me, you're doing great." I babbled, practically wanting to scream for him to slide his cock in me NOW. Whenever I'd had orgasms before, it was always centered around my cock, but this was different. I was feeling sensations I'd never felt before, encompassing my entire body.

Beads of sweat dotted Chris's forehead as he positioned his shaft at my entrance. "I'm just afraid of hurting you." He whispered, rubbing the head of his cock against me. "This isn't like anything I've done before, and I'm…"

"Please, Chris, just fuck me now." I bit my lip. I'd never felt so much desire in my life. "Make love to me, baby. I want you inside me more than anything else in the world."

Chris's hand grasped my shaft and I felt the head of his cock breaking through my seal. It felt like all the air in my lungs exhaled at once. I gasped for air, and Chris leaned over, his mouth inches from mine. "Are you okay?"

"Yeah," I breathed. "I'm okay, I know it's going to hurt the first time. Just go slow, baby, and everything will be fine." I took a deep breath, then felt more of Chris's length slide into me. My eyes fluttered shut as I grasped Chris's arms, holding onto him tight. I could feel something more than the pain, it was more emotional. For the first time ever I was truly making myself completely vulnerable to another human being. And damn, I was so happy it was with Chris.

"Are you ready for more?" Chris whispered. My eyes opened, and Chris's eyebrows were drawn together.

"Please, yes."

Chris removed his one hand from my cock and took control of my legs, positioning them on his shoulders in such a way that more of his cock went inside me.

"Yes." I sighed, and a giggle bubbled up my throat. No more pain, just these pleasurable waves flowing from my head to my toes. This wasn't just pleasure, it was happiness, bliss, and love all bound together.

Oh. My. God. Was I feeling love for Chris, or was it just the insane pleasure I felt?

I glanced up to Chris who had a smile splitting his face. He leaned over, kissed me, then began moving slowly in and out of me. His face gleamed, covered in a sheer layer of sweat. He appeared to be enjoying it, but was it anything like how I was feeling? Should I ask, or would it ruin the moment?

"Does it feel good for you too?"

"Jett, do I look like I'm in pain?" Chris bit his lower lip, then increased the pace. "This is the best moment of my life. I couldn't do this with anyone but you, because you're the only person I trust, and…" His words drifted off, a strange expression passing over his features. "I'm getting really close, Jett."

"Harder," I gasped, wanting, no, needing more. His biceps flexed with each thrust, going faster and faster until the headboard began to slap the wall behind it. Chris wrapped his fingers around my shaft, pulling on it while his face underwent a transformation. I knew that look, had seen it several times before. And now seeing the bliss emanating from him sent me over the edge.

"Oh, fuck," I gasped, and the first jet of come shot across my stomach, and I felt the muscles inside of me gripping Chris's shaft. "This, Jesus, yes, Chris, yes."

Chris glanced down at me, and his features softened for a moment. His eyes snapped shut, and his muscular frame shook as I felt his heat shooting inside of me.

Ropes of come splashed across my gut, triggered by the look on his face. Those perfect features, soon to be displayed on movie screens around the world, radiated such ecstasy.

A few moments later, once the heat had dissipated between us, Chris leaned over and brushed his lips across mine. His softening cock slipped out of me, and he fell to my side, panting for air. When we both got our breath back he threw his leg over mine and kissed the sensitive spot at the bottom of my throat.

"This was amazing." He murmured, then peppered my neck and cheeks with little kisses.

"You are amazing." I whispered, then my eyes fluttered shut and the world disappeared.

———

"What was that?"

Chris had his arm wrapped around me, my ass pushed up against his erect cock. He softly snored, pressing his erection harder against me.

"Chris, wake up. Someone's at the door."

He tightened his grip on me, then whispered, "They'll go away."

Whoever it was knocked again, and I heard Chris resume snoring. I gently disengaged myself from his arms and snuck out of bed, grabbing my robe as I left the bedroom. When I got to the door I took a deep breath and opened it.

"Huh, maybe I'm hearing things." I yawned, and when I began to shut the door I noticed a piece of paper taped to it. I pulled it off, and on the front of it Billy's name was scrawled across it. I laid it on the tiny wood table in the foyer unread and crept back to bed.

"Who was it?" Chris asked.

"Oh, sorry I woke you up." I snuggled into his arms. "Billy. I guess he's home now."

CHAPTER 23

CHRIS

I woke up in Jett's arms, and I never wanted to leave this bed. Feeling the warmth radiating off of him and the deep, steady rhythm of his breathing filled me with peace. If this could be my reality for the rest of my life I'd be the happiest man on earth.

Unfortunately, I felt a growing knot of fear in my stomach. What if I'd said too much last night? *What if Jett doesn't feel the same way that I do? If all he wants is a casual boyfriend, I don't think I can handle it.* I took a deep, steadying breath and tried to push those thoughts away.

Jett stirred, and his eyes fluttered open. "Good morning," he murmured, his voice still low and sleepy.

"Good morning," I breathed, kissing him lightly on the forehead. We lay there for a few moments in perfect contentment until he jumped out of bed.

"Oh, my God!" He exclaimed. "I have to get ready for my concert." He ran around the room searching for his clothes. "My dancing sucks, my voice sucks, shit, I'm not sure I can do this."

I reached out and took his hand, pulling him back towards me. "Hey, it's going to be fine," I tried to reassure him. "You're going to be great, and you've got hours before the show starts. Chill out and come back to bed "

Jett took a deep breath and attempted a smile. "Thanks," he says, "But you're not a critic, or a fan." Jett shook his head back and forth a few times. "I have to get there early for sound checks and other stuff."

I sighed, not wanting to let go of him. I wanted to tell Jett how I really felt, but I was still so scared. What was he thinking about besides the concert? Fuck it. If tonight was the premier of my new movie I'd be freaking out too. I take a deep breath and slowly let his fingers slide out of my hand.

"You should get ready," I said softly. "Do you have rehearsals before the show?"

"Yeah, but it's mostly the dancers. Portia and I have to warm up our voices, and I have a few interviews before it starts." Jett grabbed his clothes and jogged out of my room. I lay back on the bed, my mind spinning as I tried to process my emotions.

Last night was more than sex for me. What we did was so much more, and it made my feelings crystal clear to me – I loved Jett. And while I hoped he loved me too, I was terrified of pushing things too fast. Jett had the most important concert of his career tonight, and I couldn't spoil it.

"Coffee," I groaned, and threw my legs over the side of the bed. "I need all the caffeine this morning. And I bet Jett does too."

My legs wobbled as I stood and yawned, then I threw on my robe and padded into the kitchen. As I was making the coffee, I noticed an empty can of cat food on top of the trash.

"Oh shit, I need to take care of Kitty Purry." After the coffee maker began gurgling, I grabbed the keys for Billy's apartment and headed toward the door. That was when I noticed a note on the table in the foyer. Billy's name was written on it

"Damn it." I laughed. "I forgot, he came home last night." The paper was folded in half and taped. Apparently Jett hadn't opened it last night, so I did. I read it, then my hand flew to my chest. "What the hell does this mean?"

Dear Chris and Jett,

Thanks for watching Kitty Purry. She says you boys were the purrfect babysitters. I also want to thank you for giving me the best gift I could ever ask for.

xoxo,

Billy Higgins

What kind of present was Billy referring to? I couldn't put it together, so I decided to forget about it for now and focus on getting Jett some coffee and food.

Sticking the note in the pocket of my robe, I raced back to the kitchen, poured two cups of coffee and grabbed a couple of nearly stale bagels out of the fridge. After slicing them in half, I toasted them, put everything on a tray, and went back to Jett's bedroom.

"Please, tell me that's coffee," Jett said while tying his sneakers. His hair was still wet and I could smell the fruity scent of his shampoo.

"It is," I replied, setting the tray down on the nightstand and handing him a cup. "I wasn't sure what you'd like so I toasted bagels."

Jett smiled and grabbed one of them. His eyes sparkled as he took a bite, but then quickly dimmed as he swallowed. He set his cup down and ran a hand through his hair, messing it up even more.

"How come I can perform in front of crowds back home in Virginia, but now I'm terrified?" His voice cracked as he asked the question. I could see a hint of fear in his eyes as he waited for my answer.

I reached out and touched his arm. "It's okay to be scared," I said softly. "This isn't Virginia. It's the big time, Hollywood, and if you weren't scared I'd think something was wrong with you. Just remember why you're doing it, you know, focus on the end goal. Fame, fortune, money, and art," I pecked the tip of his nose. "And not necessarily in that order. Your voice and songs are incredible. Trust me, the audience will love you." I almost said, "I love you too," but forced myself to hold back. "Do you need your keyboards for the show? Or anything else? I have nothing going on today and I'll gladly help out if you want me to."

"No." Jett drained his coffee cup and set it on the tray. "It's a club show, so only about a thousand or so people. Clint and I recorded the backing tracks, so the only live part is my and Portia's vocals. If this was a larger venue I'd insist on more live instruments." He stood up and wrapped his arms around me. "Thanks for last night, it meant everything to me."

I shut my eyes and squeezed him tight. "It meant the world to me too, babe." I kissed him on the cheek, sparing Jett my morning breath. "You're going to be a fucking star."

––––––

"Nervous?" Hugo whispered in my ear as he hugged me. He and Becks invited me over to their house for a little party before Jett's show.

"Of course," I let him go, my nerves on edge. "If things don't go right tonight he'll be destroyed."

"Just remember, Jett's got the best voice I've heard in years." Hugo took my arm and led me to the bar. "Becks and I think tonight's going to be a massive success."

The house was buzzing with life as all of Hugo's close friends arrived. Goldie, Ram, Candace, and even Becks's agent, Frank, were here. He found us at the bar and gave me the typical Hollywood air-kisses before standing back to look me up and down. "I've heard you're Jett's new muse." Frank winked. According to Becks, Frank was a little jealous of the success Marla was having with Jett, and was coming to the show tonight to see if he wanted to get into music management.

Hugo put an arm around my shoulder and rolled his eyes. "Chris is so much more than that." he said firmly. "In fact, I think things are getting serious with you two." Hugo waggled his brows.

"Are you ready for tonight? Do you think Jett will wow everybody?" Frank asked with a raised eyebrow. The man was nice enough, but he had a sleazy showbiz vibe that got under my skin.

I faked a smile and took a sip of my drink before answering. "I'm sure of it," I said, not taking my eyes away from his intense gaze. "Jett's worked incredibly hard for this day and I know he's going to bring the house down."

"I can't wait to see Jett on stage!" Goldie's rich voice rang out. "He can't dance, but Marla played me his demos. Jett's got the pipes to make it big." She had grown on me, despite her larger-than-life persona. Tonight Goldie was wearing what she thought was a rock-and-roll outfit; a white lace tank top, tight black leather pants, and a pair of shiny blue combat boots with studs around the ankles. What made her look kinda fake was the enormous rhinestone cross hanging from her neck.

"The show starts in an hour." Becks pecked Hugo on the cheek. As always, he looked like a total star. "We'd better get going if we don't want to be late."

My phone vibrated, so I pulled it out of the pocket of my leather jacket.

"What the fuck?" I muttered. It was a Google Alert about me, and I couldn't understand the headline.

"Caught in the Act! Hilarious Kitten Photobombs Viral Celebrity Sex Tape!"

"Is everything okay?" Hugo murmured, grabbing my arm. Another alert popped up, this headline as baffling as the last.

"Sex, Lies, and Cat-titude! Unseen Paw-sibilities Unleashed in Viral Video Leak!"

"What the hell?" I clicked on the story, dread spreading through my limbs. At the top of the web page was a video link, and an article ran underneath it.

"Pawsome Intruder! Leaked Celebrity Tape Features an Adorable Cat's Unimpressed Stare!"

In a bizarre turn of events, two up and coming stars found themselves caught in a truly unforgettable moment as their intimate escapades were unexpectedly observed by a mischievous fluffy black kitten. The leaked sex tape has left the public both amused and perplexed, with the feline's photobombing antics stealing the spotlight.

The tape, which has now become the talk of Tinseltown, features Jett Sumner, the singer with mountains of buzz behind him, and Chris Reynolds, who's co-starring in Hugo Zepeda's newest flick, Bad Habits. The two stars put on a sexy show, however, what truly sets this footage apart is the presence of an adorable black kitten with radiant blue eyes, perched nonchalantly on the back of the sofa where the boys do the nasty.

As the celebrities become lost in the heat of the moment, the curious feline appears to be equally engrossed, observing their actions with an almost judgmental gaze. The kitten steals the show, effortlessly outshining the stars of the tape with its undeniable cuteness.

"It was like the kitten had a front-row seat to all the action," exclaimed one anonymous source who claimed to have viewed the leaked footage. "I laughed my ass off as it casually watched them getting down. It's like the kitten's wondering, what's all the fuss about?"

The leak is quickly becoming a viral sensation, with internet users finding ingenious ways to incorporate the fluffy feline into memes, GIFs, and cleverly edited videos.

Underneath the text was a picture of President Biden in the oval office with Kitty Purry perched on the cabinet behind his desk, judging him.

Animal behavior experts were stunned by the kitten's composure in such a compromising situation. Dr. Samantha Mathews, a renowned animal psychologist, speculated on the cat's thoughts during the event: "It's possible the kitten was in shock. Notice how his bright blue eyes never left Chris and Jett."

As the scandal continues to unfold, it seems that the photobombing kitten has inadvertently achieved overnight stardom, leaving us all to ponder the age-old question: who needs Hollywood drama when you have a fluffy feline stealing the limelight?

Suddenly I couldn't breathe. What if Jett sees this before he goes onstage?

"Are you okay, buddy?" Hugo threw his arm over my shoulder and reached down to press the link to the actual sex video, but I yanked the phone away before he could.

Tears streamed down my cheeks and I sobbed, "Marla's going to kill us!"

CHAPTER 24
JETT

"Jett, is your earpiece working?" The engineer's shrill voice carried from the back of the concert hall. "It's not giving me a signal."

"Mine's working." Portia shrugged.

I jabbed my finger into a black button on the underside of my earpiece. The rubber fit easily against my ear cushion, and Portia's voice came through clearly with no static or buzzing. "Hold on," I said. A second later I almost screamed because of the ear-splitting feedback. "Please, turn it down!" I yelled.

"I was trying to, you big baby!" The engineer snapped.

Portia jerked her earpiece out. "These things are supposed to prevent me from going deaf, not speed up the process."

"Sorry, Jett, Portia." The woman turned down the volume and Portia put the earpiece back in. "I'm turning on the click track first, then I'll cue up the first song."

Steady clicks began to play in our earpieces to the beat of our opening number. This happened before we took to the stage so we could hit the ground running and make fewer mistakes when we started singing. A moment later my opening number began and Charlie and Timothy danced onto the stage. The taped intro ended, then Portia and I ran out and began singing to the backing track.

"Sounds perfect!" The engineer cut the music. "Does it sound right to you guys?"

"Yeah," I said, nodding my head in agreement. I removed my earpiece and let it dangle around my neck. Charlie and Timothy were right behind me, looking relieved that we'd finished the sound check.

The engineer flipped a switch on her board and the entire stage lit up. "That's it then," she said with a satisfied smile. "Everything's ready for the show."

"The club is opening in ten minutes," Marla yelled from the side of the stage. "Go to the dressing room and get hydrated before the show. There's water, electrolyte drinks, and I got the pickle juice you requested, Jett."

"Pickle juice?" Portia cocked her head at me as we walked off the stage. "Yuck."

I shrugged and gave her a lopsided grin. "It works better than anything to keep you hydrated," I said. That's what the soccer coach gave us back in high school. He hated the sugary electrolyte drinks, claiming they were a poisonous mixture of dyes and sugars.

We grabbed our stuff from the side of the stage and headed towards our dressing room; a haphazard collection of crates, chairs, and a dilapidated couch that had seen better days. So much for show-business glamor.

Marla followed us into the dressing room and snatched a bottle of water out of the styrofoam cooler. "You guys, this is going to be so awesome tonight. Charlie, Timothy, do me a favor and during the chorus of all the songs, dance a little closer to Jett and Portia." She sipped her water and grinned. "Both of you have great voices, but we need to distract the crowd from noticing that neither of you can dance."

I glanced over at Portia who was already blushing from Marla's comment. I smiled at her and gave her a reassuring wink. "We'll get better," I said, making sure to emphasize the 'we'.

"Do you hear that?" Charlie asked. The thrum of voices from the growing crowd of people entering the club vibrated off the concrete walls and filled my stomach with butterflies.

"You know, guys, I've played in front of bigger crowds in Virginia. Pride festivals and raves outdoors, but I've never been this terrified." I combed my fingers through my hair, and Marla patted my shoulder.

"That's because it wasn't as important to your career. The audience tonight is filled with club kids and pop fans alike." Marla smoothed down her black sequined top. "Plus boring industry types. You'll be able to spot them because they won't be as enthusiastic. Don't perform for them, play for the real fans."

"Sorry, guys, but I need to see what's happening." Portia ducked out of the room for a moment, then all of us heard a small roar from the crowd outside. Portia raced backstage. "Jett, Marla, celebrities are showing up!"

Marla and I exchanged a glance, then raced onto the stage and pulled the curtain back an inch.

"Becks is looking especially fetching tonight," Marla winked at me, and I wondered if she had a crush on her future brother-in-law. "Oh good, he brought all our friends." She referred to Goldie, Ram, and a few other stars. When I saw Chris I practically swooned. His dark-blond hair was slicked back like a silent movie star, and I'd swear his green eyes were glowing. He wore distressed black jeans, a white wife-beater, and a leather jacket. His broad shoulders tapered down to a trim waist and long legs that were evident even under his leather jacket. A small commotion erupted around them, and a bunch of people started pointing at Chris and taking pictures.

"That's odd," I murmured.

"What?" Marla tilted her head.

"Those people in the audience recognize Chris. I mean, he hasn't even started filming *Bad Habits* yet."

"That's because I'm doing my job, getting him the right publicity." She threw her arm around my shoulder. "It's going to happen to you too."

That was when I noticed a few men in dark suits surrounding them.

"Who are those guys?" I pointed them out.

"Security," She scowled. "Hugo hates them, but he and Becks are too popular to go to clubs without at least a little muscle to protect them."

"Shit, I hope I don't ever need them."

Marla elbowed me. "You'd better hope you do. They might be pricey, but they're an indicator of success. Plus there are a lot of weirdos out there. It's better to be safe than sorry."

"Five minutes!" The stage manager's voice rang out, and Marla and I hurried back to the dressing room.

When we got there Portia was dusting her face with a glittery powder while Charlie and Timothy were doing stretches against the wall.

"Put your monitor in," I said to Portia while inserting my earpiece. She stood up and I took one last look at my reflection. My pale skin was whiter than usual, and my eyes were like saucers. Black eyeliner only accentuated it, giving me an otherworldly look I wasn't used to.

"One minute." The engineer's voice crackled through the earpiece. Portia and I looked at each other and went to the door.

"Ready, boys?" I glanced at Charlie and Timothy, who gave us a thumbs up.

The audience were shouting and clapping, and a second later the opening chords of the first song played. The four of us raced onstage and got in position. Seconds later the curtain went up, smoke and laser beams filled the air over the stage, and I sang the opening notes.

In a crowded room, our eyes first met,
A spark ignited, a feeling I can't forget,
You captured my heart with your tender gaze,
Now I'm lost in a love that's set ablaze.

Portia's voice backed mine for the last verse while I scanned the crowd for Chris. It was hard to see anything for the bright lights and the camera operators filming the show.

This world may judge us, but we'll rise above,
Two souls entwined, bound by a love so tough,
We'll break the barriers, shatter the mold,
Our love's a masterpiece, a story yet untold.

Charlie and Timothy whirled around me, and I finally found Chris in the crowd.

WTF?

Tears streamed down his cheeks, and I forced myself to look away. Then Portia took my arm and we tripped across the stage while singing the chorus.

Dancing in the moonlight, our bodies collide,
Every step we take, fills my heart with pride,
With you by my side, we'll conquer every storm,
Together we'll dance, our love forever warm.

Why the hell was Chris crying? And why was there an image of a kitten being projected on the walls of the theater?

———

"Thank you all so much!" I shouted into the mike as the final chords echoed through the club. "This has been the best night of my life!" Adrenaline raced through my body as I took my final bow.

Images of cats dotted the walls throughout the show, projected from the audience's phones. I almost asked what the hell that was about, but maybe it was some weird California thing?

"You're the best audience in the world." I took Portia's hand and held it up with mine. "Thank you very much, Goodnight!"

The show had been brilliant, as long as I didn't focus on Chris. Something was wrong with him, because he mostly kept his head down. Hugo kept his arm around him, and like Chris, appeared miserable. Becks and his celebrity friends on the other hand were dancing and singing along with me the entire show.

The curtain came down and the four of us jogged offstage. Marla stood at the side of the stage for the entire show, and when we got to her she shoved her phone in her jacket pocket and glared at me.

"Wasn't the show awesome!" Portia jumped up and down with Charlie and Timothy. A moment later they stopped, noticing the malevolent glare on Marla's face. "Did we do something wrong?" She asked, shrugging her shoulders.

"No." Marla pointed at them. "The three of you were fucking peachy. It's this one I'm pissed at." She snarled at me, then stepped forward shoving her index finger toward my face.

"You are so fucking fired." Marla threw her hands up in the air, exasperated. "Do you know how much money the record company is going to lose because you can't keep your dick in your pants?"

"What, wha..."

"And fucking Chris." She ran her hands through her hair

and growled. "If the studio doesn't fire him, I'll be shocked. Neither of you thought for one minute how your..."

"Wait!" I held up my hand. "What are you talking about?"

Marla crossed her arms over her chest and shook her head slowly back and forth. Then she pulled her phone out and handed it to me. The screen was filled with images of me and Chris, naked.

"What the hell is this?" I gasped. A headline underneath it confused the hell out of me.

"Purr-plexing Scandal! Celebrities' Steamy Video Takes an Unexpected Feline Twist!"

Marla snatched the phone back, spun around and stalked off. When she got to the stage door she turned around, shot me the bird and screamed.

"You're fired!"

CHAPTER 25
CHRIS

My eyes fluttered open for what seemed the hundredth time since Jett and I went to bed last night, and this time, I didn't try to go back to sleep. What was the point? My overactive and stressed brain couldn't be turned off.

"Mom," Jett whimpered in his sleep. I pulled him in closer to me, and wished I could clap my hands, wake him up, and tell him that last night was only a dream. But after the events of yesterday, I felt bad for thinking about trying to wake him

Jett didn't remove his stage makeup before going to sleep, and his black eyeliner was so smudged he reminded me of an exceptionally handsome trash panda. But at least one of us was getting some sleep.

The little bit of sleep I got was littered with horrifying dreams. The worst one had me and Jett starring in a porno directed by filthy Billy. In it the director kept saying, "This is the only work you can get now, so get busy sucking my cock!"

I shuddered, and Jett's eyes opened. A single tear leaked out of his left eye, leaving a black streak running down the side of his nose. "Mommy," he said in a tiny voice, and I knew that he was still shaken up by the dream.

I hugged him close and stroked his hair. I wanted to tell him that everything was going to be okay, but I couldn't bring myself to do it because I wasn't sure if it was true or not. We were in an uncertain moment with no clear answers in sight.

"Babe, it was just a dream." I kissed the top of his head, and he shifted so he could look up to my face. "Please, tell me last night was a dream," Jett muttered, reaching up and swiping his tears away. "A fucking nightmare."

"It was." I sighed, then both of our phones pinged at once. Jett sat up, reached for the nightstand to grab his cell, then thought better of it and snuggled closer to me.

"What are we going to do now?" Jett asked, and I wondered if I should even attempt an answer. "Pack it in? Go back to boring old Richmond?"

"And be forced to tell everyone how we fucked everything up?" I murmured. "I don't want to face our friends and families. Jesus, my parents are going to have a cow. I'm sure there's someplace where nobody's heard of us before."

Jett hissed the words, "They don't call it the world wide web for nothing." His eyes narrowed into slits. "Maybe there's a cave on an island in the middle of the ocean we can hide in." His voice was a ragged snarl, full of fear and anger. "When I get my hands on Billy I'm going to teach the old perv a lesson."

When we arrived home last night I had to physically restrain Jett from tearing down Billy's door. While I was fucking pissed at the man too, violence would only feed the rumor mills. As far as I was concerned, me and Jett needed to lie low and pray that a new scandal would pop up. Hopefully to an actual star instead of two extremely minor celebs.

One of our phones rang again. "Jett, we can't ignore the

world forever." I reached over him and snatched my phone up. "Fuck, it's my parents."

"Don't answer it." Jett tried to take the phone away.

"Look, if we don't face the music now, it's going to get worse." I gritted my teeth and answered. "Hello?"

"Chris Reynolds, what on earth are you thinking making X-rated videos?" Mom's voice was so loud I held the phone away from my ear. Jett sat up next to me, listening in. "The Richmond Times Dispatch has left over a dozen messages, and so has Style Weekly. If your intention was to hurt and humiliate me and your father, consider it a job well done." Mom screamed the last few words.

"Mom, I swear we didn't..."

"Give me that phone," I heard Dad growl. "Son, we've put up with you wanting to be an actor, or whatever it is you think you're doing, but this is the limit."

Jett's phone started ringing. He grabbed it, cringed, then put it back.

"I called out sick from work today because I can't, no, *I won't* answer questions about my sleazy son and his fucking boyfriend." Dad sighed dramatically. "We have no problems with you being gay, but we'd prefer it if you didn't do it in front of a fucking camera!"

I hung up and placed my phone next to Jett's.

"There's no point trying to talk to them right now, it's too soon." I sighed, then turned to Jett and attempted a smile. "Hey, no matter what happens, I want us to stay together."

"It'll take a crowbar to wrench me off of you." Jett rubbed his eyes, and I couldn't help but laugh. "What's so funny?"

"Nothing. Everything. Shit, what a fucked-up place Holly-wood is." I got out of bed, ran to the bathroom, and returned with a handheld mirror. "You forgot to take your makeup off last night." I handed it to Jett, who took one look then pulled the covers over his head.

"Oh my God, I look so awful." He whined. "It looks like somebody beat the shit out of me."

I got back in bed and pulled the blankets over my head too. There was just enough light filtered through the blankets that we could see each other. "You don't look awful, or beat up." I pecked him on the lips. "Maybe a little worse for wear, but I love you anyways."

Jett froze.

I stared at him, my heart pounding in my chest. I hadn't realized I'd said it out loud until he responded. Somehow that felt bigger than if I had planned to tell him. His gaze was fierce and intense and my stomach dropped as the moments dragged on.

Jett finally blinked and let out a shaky breath. "That's… that's a lot to take in," he murmured, his voice still thick with emotion. "It's getting hot under here." Jett pulled the blanket off of us and continued staring at me. "But," he continued, looking up at me with those racoon eyes, "It's also kind of amazing." A small but genuine smile lit up his face.

My heart swelled and I reached out for his hand, entwining our fingers together. "Do you, you know, feel the same?"

Jett bit his lower lip and nodded. "Yeah, I do. Chris, I love you. You're the only man I've met who makes me feel this way. No matter what happens to us, I never want to leave your side."

My cheeks warmed and I found myself grinning like an idiot as I leaned forward and pressed our lips together. In my head, my inner child was jumping up and down, screaming, "HE LOVES ME! HE REALLY LOVES ME!"

When the kiss broke, Jett asked, "So what now?"

I raised an eyebrow. "Now we figure out how to survive this whole media crap without going crazy."

Jett reached for his phone, then pulled his hand back. "We need to figure out what's going on, but I'm afraid to look."

Both of our phones pinged. Jett's lips twisted, and I could tell he was forcing back laughter. Jesus, our lives were so fucked. A giggle bubbled up my throat, and a second later we cracked up, holding on to each other as the stress of the prior twenty-four hours finally had a release. Finally Jett grabbed his phone. He scanned the screen for a moment then held it so I could see it. On it were dozens of notifications from various gossip sites and tabloids with headlines that had grown oh so familiar.

"Cat-astrophe Caught on Tape: Feline Friend Witnesses Surprising Encounter Between Chris Reynolds and Jett Sumner"

"They need to come up with more original headlines," Jett grumbled.

"Secrets Revealed: Chris Reynolds and Jett Sumner's Leaked Video Shakes Hollywood, But a Curious Kitten Adds a Whisker of Intrigue"

I took the phone from Jett, pecked him on the cheek and climbed out of bed. "Have you ever thought this might turn out okay? Like, haven't you heard that any publicity, no matter how awful it might be, is actually good PR?" I pulled on a robe and went to the door. "I desperately need coffee. Do you want breakfast? I'll bring it to you in bed."

"No, I've gotta wash the makeup off." Jett stood and put on his robe. "I look like..."

There was a knock at the door, and we both froze.

"What if it's a reporter?" I whispered. "It's not like this is a high security building."

"Just look through the peephole first." Jett whispered back, and we both crept out of the bedroom. Whoever it was knocked again.

"Chris, Jett, it's me, Billy!"

Jett's hands balled into fists and he raced for the door.

"Wait, Jett, don't do something you'll regret!" I grabbed his shoulder which he immediately shrugged off. With shaking hands he unlocked the deadbolt and glared at Filthy Billy.

"What the fuck did you do to us?"

CHAPTER 26

JETT

illy spun around and raced for his door. I grabbed him by the shoulder and hauled him into our apartment.

"Please, don't hurt me. I'm sorry, I swear to God I'm sorry!" He babbled, and Chris shut the door behind us. I let go of Filthy Billy and pointed to the sofa in the living room.

"Sit your ass down now." I barked, and he shuffled over to the sofa. Once he was sitting, it was hard to be angry because of how pathetic he looked. As usual he was wearing all neon colors. He wore a lime green mesh t-shirt with nothing underneath it, and hot pink shorts with a banana print. He hadn't touched up his roots so there was half-an-inch of white hair sprouting from his scalp, and he hadn't bothered to color his pencil-thin mustache. Damn it, he looked like a vulnerable old man.

"Meow."

"Did you hear that?" Chris cocked an eyebrow and went to the door. A second later Kitty Purry bounded into the room and jumped on Billy's lap.

"Oh, baby, I'm so sorry to leave you with these mean guys." Billy held the kitten under his chin, and you could hear her purrs from across the room. I paced in front of them while Chris went to the bathroom. He came back and handed me a couple of wipes.

"Your eyes." He whispered. I grimaced and began wiping last night's makeup off. Jesus, living in Hollywood made everyone hyper aware of appearances. "The way things are going, reporters might show up or something."

"Billy, what in God's name possessed you to film us?" I spat. "Do you have any idea how badly you've messed up by taking that video to the press?" I tossed a used wipe on the coffee table, my face twisted with rage.

"I, I swear, I didn't show it to the press." Billy's voice quivered.

"Then how on earth did every Hollywood gossip rag find out about it?" Chris crossed his arms over his chest and glared at him.

Billy's eyes darted around the room before settling on a spot on the wall. "You two must have turned on my camera by mistake." he mumbled. His voice was so quiet I almost didn't catch it. "When I returned home I noticed it wasn't positioned the way it normally is. So I checked it out to make sure it wasn't damaged."

"Kitty Purry," Chris mumbled. "Remember when we heard that crash and found the camera knocked over?" He sighed dramatically. "We found the camera on the floor, and she was under it, I think. I must've switched the damned thing on when I picked it up."

"There was also my security cam." Billy's forehead was covered in a sheen of sweat. "When I discovered the footage you two shot, it was incomplete, so I..."

"What do you mean?" I sat across from the old man,

clutching the armrest of the chair so I wouldn't take a swing at him.

"On the video it shows you two rummaging through my supplies, then..." Billy began, and Chris cut him off.

"What supplies?"

"You know, lube, condoms, dildos, that kind of stuff." Billy attempted a smile. "I'd like the lube back. It's the expensive kind."

Chris and I both rolled our eyes.

Billy pierced me with an accusing glare, his words slicing through the air like a hot knife. "You guys pretend to be so naive. Don't tell me you don't even know what a ball gag is."

I slammed my hands on the armrests, fury bubbling up inside me. "Enough!" I shouted, my patience unraveling. "Just spit out your damn story already."

Billy's eye twitched, then he let out a long sigh. "Fine. You boys were messing around with my belongings, then you both got on my couch. The camera angle was messed up so I couldn't see everything, since you didn't put the camera back properly. So I examined my security footage and pieced the two together. Why the hell couldn't you two virgins go all the way on video?" Billy shook his head sadly. "You guys left, taking the lube with you. When I got home, I put all the pieces together, and decided to put the video up on my website. How was I to know you boys already have fans?"

"What do you mean?" Chris asked.

"I gave you both fake names on my website. That means people recognized you both and reported it to the gossip sites." Billy shrugged. "If you're going to come into my home and have sex, I'm within my rights to make money off of it."

My eyes snapped shut and I struggled to remain calm. Who the fuck did he think he was, filming us without our knowledge?

"You're right," Chris murmured, and I opened my eyes and scowled. "We shouldn't have gone through your stuff, and we're sorry." Chris sighed, then shook his head. "What can we say to get you to remove the video from..."

There was a knock at the door.

"Can this day get any worse?" Chris ambled to the front door as if he were moving through water.

"Our families saw those videos, Billy." I said, my stomach clenching. "My career is over before it's even started."

"We came over as soon as we could." Hugo strolled into the living room, his arm around Chris. Becks followed along behind them. "I've tried to talk sense into Marla, but she's totally freaked out."

"Hi, Hugo." Filthy Billy offered Hugo a weak smile. Then he saw Becks and must've had an inner starstruck moment. His smile brightened for a quick second, then faded as all of us scowled at him.

"Aww, look at the kitty." Hugo got on his knees in front of Billy and took Kitty Purry from him. He rubbed his cheek against the kitten, then he held the kitty up and smiled. "Oh! You're the famous kitty from the video!"

"Jesus fucking Christ!" I leapt to my feet. "This man has ruined my and Chris's careers. What the hell can we do to fix this? And for God's sake. Is there anyone in fucking Tinsel Town who hasn't see the damned video?"

"Eww." Chris made a face. "I can't believe my best friend watched me lose my virginity."

"Seriously?" Becks backed up a step. "You two were virgins? Because it looked like you knew exactly what you were doing."

Chris sank onto the couch next to me and buried his face in my chest. "I can't believe everyone we know watched that video." His shoulders heaved and I realized he was crying.

"It's okay, baby." I wrapped my arms around him. "We didn't

lose our virginities on camera, remember? We came back to the apartment for that."

"It doesn't matter." Chris sobbed. "That was a private moment. I didn't want the whole world to see it."

All eyes were glued on us, and for the first time Billy appeared remorseful.

"Just leave," I croaked. "All of you, get out. Can't we have at least a little privacy?"

'I'm so sorry," Becks murmured, his eyes shifting to the floor. "It was wrong for us to look at..." He didn't finish his sentence because of a knock at the door. Nobody moved or said a word, and whoever it was knocked again.

"Chris! Jett! It's me, Marla. Please, open the door."

"Shit." Chris murmured. He glanced up and swiped at his wet red face. "Hugo, will you let her in please?"

Hugo gave the kitten back to Billy and hurried to the door. When Marla strolled into the living room she stopped in her tracks as soon as she saw us.

"Jesus, you guys look like shit." She sighed. "And it's my fault. I shouldn't have abandoned you at Catch One, Jett. It's just I..."

"You're right, you shouldn't have." I stood and pointed at her. "And by the way, if anyone's going to fire anyone, it's us." I placed my hand on Chris's shoulder. "You work for me and Chris, not the other way around. If you ever pull a stunt like that again, I'll take you to court for breach of contract."

Marla blanched. "May I sit, please?"

I shrugged, and Marla sat next to Filthy Billy. "What a cute kitten!"

She tried to pet Kitty Purry on her head, and the kitten bit her. "Ouch! You fucking little..."

"You deserve it." Chris snarled.

"I'm truly sorry, guys." Marla stuck her index finger in her mouth. When she pulled it out there was a spot of blood. "Look, I overreacted. One of my cardinal rules as an agent is to avoid porn at all costs. When I saw the video I had a meltdown." She stuck a strand of hair in her mouth, and for a moment I imagined her as a teenage girl. "This morning I got a call from the record company."

"They dropped me, right?" I mumbled, past the point of giving a damn.

"No, oh my God. Your single, which was released only yesterday, is in the top thirty already. It's had over a million streams, and if this keeps up they think it'll be top ten." Marla grinned. "This is surpassing all expectations. And I'm not talking about the dance chart, I'm talking about the Billboard 100. The Big Daddy of the charts!"

"Oh." Reality settled on my shoulders. "My song's a hit?" My heart hammered in my chest. Chris turned and grinned at me.

"You're gonna be a star." He winked. "But what about me? Is the studio freaking out?" Chris glared at Marla.

"No, not at all." Marla barked out a laugh. "They love the publicity." She attempted to pet Kitty Purry again, who hissed at her. "This angry little fluff ball looks like the cat in the video." She froze, and if this was a cartoon, a lightbulb would have blazed over her head. "Wait a second. It wasn't your apartment in the video Chris, and you don't own a cat."

"This is Kitty Purry, and the boys were filmed in my apartment." Billy grinned, while I, Chris, Hugo, and Becks all sucked in our breaths. Shit was about to hit the fan.

Marla's face contorted in rage as she screamed, "It was you?!" Jumping to her feet, she pointed an accusing finger. "I'm going to sue you until you don't have a penny to your name! How dare you intrude on my clients' rights and privacy by filming them without their knowledge or consent!"

Kitty Purry's growl echoed through the air like a rattlesnake's warning rattle, her fur standing on end.

"Don't even think about it! Nobody messes with Billy Higgins!" Billy shouted.

"Don't fuck with my sister, you scumbag." Hugo got to his feet, glaring down at the old man. "And what the hell were you thinking filming my best friends having sex?"

"Hugo, do you want me to have my lawyer handle this?" Becks whipped out his phone and started typing.

As everyone argued, it dawned on me that everything had worked out in our favor. Did I like the fact that people around the globe were watching me have an intimate moment with Chris, the man I loved? No. But I loved having a hit single, and if whipping my dick out helped my career...

"Hey," Chris whispered, taking my hand. "Let's get out of here."

"I'm going to kill you, old man!" Marla shrieked, then reached into her purse. Billy's hand flew to his chest. She pulled out a bottle of mace and aimed it at him.

"You'll regret the day you were born, you fucking bitch!" Billy screamed, and Becks got in between them.

"C'mon." I took Chris's hand. While everyone argued, I led Chris to the door. "I can't believe we're sneaking out of our own apartment." I whispered, opening the door.

Chris pulled me through it. When the door shut he pulled me in close and smiled. "I love you, Jett."

Wow. This had to be the most intense twenty-four hours of my life. I now had a hit single, a celebrity sex-tape scandal, and the man I was in love with loved me too.

"I love you too, Chris." I felt like my heart would burst in my chest. "More than anyone else in the world."

EPILOGUE
CHRIS- ONE YEAR LATER

The room was buzzing as our agent Marla barked out orders. Cameras were rolling and sound equipment was being tested. Our families were arranged in a semicircle, seated in matching armchairs.

"No, Jett, sit in the chair next to your mother. It shows off your profile better." Marla commanded, and Mom sniffed. When Marla wasn't in the same room with us, Mom called her the She-Devil. "Chris, sit in between your parents. It's uncanny how much you look like your Dad."

I felt a mixture of annoyance and pride as I settled into the chair. It was true; I was the spitting image of my father, but our temperaments couldn't be more opposite. I loved him, but sometimes it was hard.

The sound technician adjusted the levels on his equipment, and I suddenly realized what this meant: in a few minutes, I'd be on national television. Again. My heart pounded as I gripped the armrest of my chair. I'd been through countless interviews over the last year, and you'd think I'd be used to it by now. But it was never easy, and now that our folks were being interviewed with us, both me and Jett were terrified.

"Bless her heart," Mom whispered in my ear. "You should tell your agent to lay off the caffeine. She's so snippy." She smoothed out her blue-green kilt and faked a smile. My parents were old school preppy Virginians who thought Marla was a prime example of decadent Hollywood.

"It's not caffeine Mom." I whispered back. "She quit smoking." Mom used to be a smoker, so I thought maybe she'd have a little empathy.

"Poor dear." Mom crossed her legs. "How long ago did she quit?"

"Um, well, it was a little over a year ago, I think." If I recalled correctly, I'd never seen her smoke, but she was constantly chewing nicotine gum. "She's addicted to the gum."

"Hello everyone, thanks for being here." Lainey Turner, the host of Here's Hollywood! strolled into the living room with an assistant on her heels. "It's a pleasure meeting all of you." She sat in an antique Chippendale chair that had been in our family for generations. When I was a kid I'd pretended it was a throne, and I was the king of America. A sound tech handed her an earpiece and helped arrange it around her enormous red hairdo.

"Chris, her face doesn't move." Mom whispered, and I saw Jett's Mom whispering to him at the same time. Most likely saying the same thing. Our families had known each other for years, but now that Jett and I were a couple, they'd become tight friends. Most weekends they'd play tennis together at Westwood Racquet Club before getting hammered in the club lounge. Most likely they drank away the embarrassment of having out and proud celebrity sons. In their circles, being famous was only a good thing if you won a Pulitzer prize, or a political race. Despite their reservations, they'd become vocal supporters of us.

"If you're not on camera, get off the set now!" The director shouted. Marla scowled and jogged away, settling next to the dining room door. "Lainey, we're ready in five, four, three, two, one, action!"

"This is Lainey Turner coming to you live from the childhood home of actor and model Chris Reynolds in Richmond, Virginia." A broad smile stretched across her extra plump cheeks. "His partner Jett Sumner is with us, along with both of their parents. In a shocking move, Chris and Jett are moving back to their hometown. Tell us Jett, why the sudden change?"

Jett smiled for the camera. "We missed Richmond, and our families. While we love Hollywood, we feel more at home here. We still have a place in Santa Monica that we live in when we are working there."

He glanced fondly at me as he spoke, and his mother tittered with approval. "We also love the slower pace of life here," he continued. I couldn't help but chuckle, thinking of all the times Jett and I were chased by papparazzi. Why make it easy for them by living in Hollywood?

"Yes, absolutely." Lainey nodded sternly. "But what about your career? Will you still be able to pursue it from Richmond?"

"Of course," I nodded. "When I'm not in LA, I'm usually in New York or Europe modeling." After making Bad Habits, I'd become the spokesman for Laurent Delacroix, an upscale men's designer. "Richmond is a peaceful place for us, and we get to be closer to our families.

"As a musician I'm not tied to any location." Jett shrugged. "Our new home has a state of the art recording studio, and it overlooks the James River. It's very peaceful which helps my creative process."

What he wasn't saying was how the Hollywood publicity machine kills his creativity. Thanks, Marla. Not.

"Mr. and Mrs. Reynolds, I'm sure you're thrilled to have Chris back." Lainey smiled, and my mother's fake smile spread across her face.

"Chris is a delight, and of course we're so happy for Jett too." Mom patted my knee. "The four of us," Mom gestured toward Jett's folks, "visited Hollywood a few months ago to see our boys. While it's a lovely city, Chris and Jett were constantly stressed by their, um, work." Mom coughed and shot a look at Marla.

"Let's hear from your parents, Jett." Lainey glanced over to the teleprompter. "How did you react when the gay sex tape scandal happened?"

Jett's parents exchanged a look, and his father cleared his throat. "It was a shock, of course," he said. "We were horrified that someone would do something so vile to our son and Chris."

Jett glanced away, embarrassed.

Jett's mother laid a hand on her husband's arm. "But we couldn't be more proud of how Jett handled the situation with grace and dignity. He and Chris worked together to mitigate the damage, and they've both come out stronger on the other side."

"You all took it in stride," Lainey replied. She gestured to me. "Chris, what have you learned since the scandal?"

To trust absolutely no one in Hollywood was the honest answer. Instead, I gave an answer I'd rehearsed plenty of times with Marla. "I've learned that no one is invincible -- even celebrities can be vulnerable to attack from outside sources," I said quietly. This speech was a steaming pile of kitty turds. "But we all have inner strength that helps us get through difficult times. It's important to recognize it in yourself and trust in it."

Jett snickered.

Lainey nodded her agreement. "Very inspiring words," she said before glancing back at the teleprompter for her next question. "So what does the future hold for Chris Reynolds and Jett Sumner?"

"I have a new album dropping in three months, then I'm going on a world tour. Until then, I'll be decorating our new home and reconnecting with friends and family." Jett laid his arm over his mother's shoulder.

"New York Fashion week is coming up, and I will start shooting a new film in Charleston, South Carolina next year." I replied, winking at Jett.

We were purposely leaving out the biggest news of all. Jett and I were flying our families to Hawaii in two weeks for a secret wedding. The Hollywood press would mostly leave us alone while we lived in Virginia, and wouldn't suspect a thing. Everyone involved was sworn to secrecy. Hell, we hadn't even told Marla yet. Thank God Hugo and Becks were in Canada working on a new film together. If gossip was an Olympic sport, Hugo would win the gold.

After a few more questions, Lainey ended the interview. "Thanks Jett, Chris, and your wonderful parents for spending time with us today."

"It's a wrap," the director called out, and all of us sighed with relief.

"There's food in the dining room for everyone." Mom grinned and gestured toward the adjoining room. Mom was the perfect hostess, and insisted on providing food for the Hollywood heathens, as she called them. The long mahogany table was laden with ham biscuits, chicken salad sandwiches from Ukrops, and some kind of orange jello mold with marshmallows and nuts.

"Let's get out of here for a minute," Jett whispered, then took my hand and dragged me to the backdoor.

I opened the door and a chill breeze made me shiver. "Just for a minute. The only thing I miss about LA is the weather."

We leaned against the wood railing of the deck and put our arms around each other. A couple of rabbits saw us and scurried under the wooden fence surrounding the property.

"Do you ever regret moving to Hollywood?" I murmured. "I mean now, after discovering what life without privacy is truly like?"

"Of course not," Jett snuggled closer. "We're truly privileged to have the life that we do. But yeah, the lack of privacy sucks. Like, why is it important for fans of our work to know everything about us? When that photographer followed us into the men's room in New York it took every ounce of self-control not to beat the shit out of him."

"Which is why we've come home. Hopefully we'll be able to work and live in peace." I kissed his cheek. "Though anywhere on the planet with you is home to me."

"I love you, Chris."

"And I love you more."

The End

———

The following is a preview of the novel The Cad & Dad, the first novel in the Southern Discomfort series.

I'd first gone to see Cris Foster when Brian filed for divorce. She'd had a calming effect on me, and helped me realize that I was in charge of my emotional well-being, not my ex-husband. Before I started therapy, I thought seeing a therapist was a waste of time. What kept me going back to her was silly, but I was glad I stuck it out. Her name was the same as my favorite character on The Young And The Restless, a soap opera my granny and I watched together when I was a kid. It was a stupid reason, but watching the stories, as my granny called them, was the beginning of my love affair with telling stories of my own.

Blue Ridge Pride Behavioral Associates was in a plain, one-story brick house on the other side of Asheville. There were only three therapists and a receptionist. A trans friend who found their help invaluable had referred me to them as he was transitioning. After three years of weekly visits I announced that I felt healed enough to stop coming. Now I was back with my tail between my legs.

As I stepped out of my SUV onto the gravel driveway, the front door opened and a woman stepped out, tears streaming down her face. My first instinct was to comfort her, but when she saw me she covered her face with her hand and ran to her car.

"God, am I so confused about my life that I want to reopen old wounds?" I muttered, then forced myself to move. Suddenly, I remembered being that woman. Reliving every drama Brian and I had gone through. But, it was worth it in the end. We might have been divorced, but Brian and I kept our friendship and business arrangements going, thanks to Cris.

"Thatch, it's good to see you again!" The receptionist said when I walked through the door. His name was Tim, and he also taught yoga and reiki at the new age bookstore downtown.

"Hey Tim." I grinned. When I was about to sit on the tattered overstuffed sofa, he stopped me.

"Thatch, I forgot to ask you this on the phone. Are you allergic to dogs? Because Cris now has an emotional support dog that sits in on the sessions."

"Oh, really? I love dogs. Can't wait to meet..."

"Her name is Harmony, and you'll love her. She's been helpful for certain patients, and hopefully Harmony will be a comfort to you as well." Tim said, then placed his hands together like he was praying, and bowed his head. "Cris is ready for you."

"Oh, that was fast," I replied. "Is she still in the same office?"

"Cris's office is at the end of the hallway, the one with the dreamcatcher hanging on the door." He pointed toward her office. "Just walk on in, she's expecting you."

Hanging from her door was a hoop with what appeared to be crude netting inside of it. Bird feathers and brightly colored beads were woven into it. When I opened the door it appeared smoky inside, and an overpowering smell of musk roared up my nostrils.

"Thatch, it's lovely to see you again." Cris beamed at me, and then I saw the source of the smoke. Incense was burning in an elaborate brass thingy, and I recalled how Cris always kept it burning, saying it helped cleanse the spirit.

"You look the same," I commented. Her long brown hair was in a single braid hanging over her left shoulder, and she still had the same granny glasses, similar to the ones John Lennon wore. I held out my hand and she took it in hers, but instead of shaking it, she held it in both hands and shut her eyes.

"I can sense your anxiety," Cris murmured, then opened her eyes and released my hand. "You're in a safe space. Let's begin the healing process." She gestured toward the blue velvet antique couch across from her desk, so I sat. "Let me introduce you to the newest member of Blue Ridge Pride Behavioral Associates, Harmony."

A gorgeous long-haired black chihuahua crawled out from under the couch and stared at me. "Go ahead," Cris directed me. "Pick her up. She loves cuddles."

I leaned over and set her on my lap. Then the little darling got on her hind feet with her paws on my chest and licked my chin. "Aww, what a sweet girl." After the kiss, Harmony curled up on my lap. "What a wonderful way to put your clients at ease."

"Harmony is a rescue. My wife Amber found her at the animal shelter and couldn't resist bringing her home." Amber was one of the therapists working here. "Normally she lives up to her name, but today she got a little feisty with me."

"It's hard to believe this little bundle of fluff could be a bad girl." I cooed while Harmony licked my fingers.

"It's understandable why, so all is forgiven. The vet cancelled her appointment today, so I had to go on YouTube and look up videos on how to express a dog's anal gland." She threw her hands up in the air. "Poor Harmony was past due for it. I managed to get the job done, and saved a ton of money too."

I glanced down at my hands, the ones Cris had just held in her own. Harmony tilted her tiny head, a questioning look in her eyes. I scanned the room, praying there was a bottle of hand sanitizer somewhere, but there wasn't.

"It was a lot more difficult than I thought. But Harmony is a trooper. So what's going on with you, Thatch?" Cris asked, picking lint from the sleeve of her lavender turtleneck. "The last time we spoke you felt at peace with your ex-husband."

It took a moment for me to get my thoughts together. On the ride here I'd gone over everything I wanted to say, but after learning about Harmony's anal gland it had all flown out of my head.

Cris stared at me with a neutral expression that had always made me feel like I wasn't being judged, while I struggled to get my brain to work. "Dating. Men. Um, there's something wrong with me." I mumbled.

"Go on." Cris murmured, her eyes not leaving mine. "Remember, this is a safe space. Feel free to share whatever you need to."

"I'm fifty-one years old, and I've been divorced for several years. But in all that time I haven't gone on a single date. Finally, a man asked me out, and I'm terrified." I blurted, and Harmony dug into my crotch with her rear leg.

"How does this man make you feel?"

I nudged Harmony to get her to stop kicking my junk, shut my eyes and pictured Joey's face. "He's handsome, with shoulder-length brown hair, and he works as a nurse. But, he's much younger than I am."

"I asked how you felt about him, but you still said something interesting. Do you have issues with this age gap?" Cris asked, and I waved a cloud of smoke out of my face.

"Well, yeah. In my head I know it shouldn't be a problem, but…"

"But, it is." Cris said, a nun's smile settling on her face. "Are you attracted to this man?"

"Kind of?" I mumbled. What did I think about him? It wasn't like I was gaga over Joey. "When I met Brian, my ex-husband, I immediately felt something for him." I laced my fingers through Harmony's hair and began stroking her. "Actually, Brian pissed me off when we first met, but I can't remember what it was."

Cris raised an eyebrow.

"Oh, I remember. It was his attitude. A few weeks later and I couldn't imagine life without him, but Joey is different. He's very nice, good-looking, and, you know, nice." I shrugged my shoulders, wishing I could explain the doubt I felt. Hell, I was a best-selling author, but the correct words escaped me.

"Something is holding you back, right?" Cris asked, then pointed at the coffee table in front of me. "See that piece of obsidian?"

"Um, what is that?"

"It's that shiny piece of black glass. Pick it up and hold it in your hands." I did as instructed, and Harmony growled when I bent over. "Obsidian is a crystal that aids in healing. It possesses energies that help you process emotions. Can you feel the power?"

It felt heavy and smooth, but that was about it. I nodded yes anyway. Who knows? Maybe it was doing something and I was too skeptical to feel it.

"Close your eyes, Thatch."

I did as instructed, and was startled when I heard what sounded like a gong.

"Focus, Thatch." Cris's voice deepened. "How do you actually feel about the man who asked you on a date?"

"Nothing," I blurted. "Like, he's a nice guy, but I feel nothing. He's taking care of the pain in my ass that's living upstairs, so I guess I feel gratitude for his, um, presence."

"You just mentioned that a so-called pain in the ass is living upstairs from you." Cris said, and I opened my eyes. "I'm assuming it means a person."

I nodded.

"Does this person have a name?" Cris asked, and I realized I was still rubbing the stupid glass rock. I set it back on the coffee table, and Harmony growled again.

"Cary Lancaster," I sighed. "He's this guy my son brought home." How the hell could I describe this man and the chaos he'd brought to my life? "To make a long story short, Cary had a medical emergency and he's recuperating in Sam's bedroom. I would send him packing, but his doctor insists on keeping him close by the hospital."

Cris steepled her hands under her chin and shut her eyes for a moment. When she opened them, she asked, "So, this man infuriates you?"

"God yes. Cary is a pompous, stuck-up rich guy who thinks the world revolves around him. He even drives a Rolls Royce. Like, who the hell does that unless you want to flaunt your privilege to the world?" I snapped.

Harmony yipped, then jumped off my lap and scampered

under the couch. Cris scribbled something, then pursed her lips. She opened her mouth, shut it again, then spoke.

"Maybe you should reconsider why you are here, Thatch, because it sounds to me like Cary is the source of your angst."

———

ABOUT THE AUTHOR

Ian O. Lewis is a bestselling author of LGBTQ fiction and romance. Originally from Richmond, Virginia, he now calls Mexico home. Follow him on social media, Amazon, and Bookbub to keep up to date with new books, his life in Mexico, and the sordid things that keeps him up at night.

ALSO BY IAN O. LEWIS

The Boys of Oregon Hill Series

Lovefool

Recreational Love

Mr. Mouthful

Handsy

The Boundary

The Balcony Boys Duet

Situationship

Max

The Making It Series

Making It Fit

Making It Spark

Making It Sizzle

Making It Glitter

Making It Legal

The Southern Discomfort Series

The Cad & Dad

Inconveniently Yours

Suddenly Single

Hollywood Hearts Series

The Big One

Standalone Novels

Serve

Missionary

Writing as Luke Jameson

Confessions: Justin's Penance, Lust & Ecstasy

Gay4Pay- The Complete Series

Ingram Content Group UK Ltd.
Milton Keynes UK
UKHW020649050623
422889UK00016B/1727